Tama had his arms right around her, and it took a moment for Mikki to realise she was clinging to his neck as he trod water out in the middle of the dive pool. She tried to answer but couldn't speak yet. She tried to move but Tama's hold tightened.

'Be still,' he advised calmly. 'Get your breath back.'

There was something so gentle in that command to 'be still' that Mikki found herself transfixed. Almost hypnotised.

Their heads were so close.

Close enough to kiss.

Where had *that* come from? Involuntarily, Mikki's gaze dropped to Tama's mouth, and desire hit somewhere deep in her belly with the kick of a mule. He had the most *kissable* mouth she'd ever seen. Lips that looked so soft but had such firm lines. Lines that were currently crooked, with one side pulled up into the hint of a smile.

Mikki's gaze shot up to find Tama watching her very steadily. His gaze dropped to *her* mouth.

Oh...Lord! Had he guessed what she'd been thinking about? And the way he was looking back at her now...was it possible he'd been thinking the same thing?

Yes.

Alison Roberts lives in Christchurch, New Zealand. She began her working career as a primary school teacher, but now juggles available working hours between writing and active duty as an ambulance officer. Throwing in a large dose of parenting, housework, gardening and pet-minding keeps life busy, and teenage daughter Becky is responsible for an increasing number of days spent on equestrian pursuits. Finding time for everything can be a challenge, but the rewards make the effort more than worthwhile.

Recent titles by the same author:

THE ITALIAN SURGEON'S CHRISTMAS MIRACLE
MARRYING THE MILLIONAIRE DOCTOR*
HER FOUR-YEAR BABY SECRET
THE ITALIAN SURGEON CLAIMS HIS BRIDE
CHRISTMAS BRIDE-TO-BE
THE PLAYBOY DOCTOR'S PROPOSAL*

Crocodile Creek

ONE NIGHT
WITH HER BOSS

BY
ALISON ROBERTS

MILLS & BOON™
Pure reading pleasure™

All the characters in this book have no existence outside the imagination of the author, and have no relation whatsoever to anyone bearing the same name or names. They are not even distantly inspired by any individual known or unknown to the author, and all the incidents are pure invention.

First published in Great Britain 2009
Harlequin Mills & Boon Limited,
Eton House, 18-24 Paradise Road, Richmond, Surrey TW9 1SR

© Alison Roberts 2009

ISBN: 978 0 263 86836 4

Set in Times Roman 10½ on 12¼ pt
03-0409-45632

Printed and bound in Spain
by Litografia Rosés, S.A., Barcelona

ONE NIGHT
WITH HER BOSS

CHAPTER ONE

'I WON'T do it.'

'Won't do what? Hey, wait up, Tama!'

Tama James covered his head with a determined shove of his helmet. He scowled at his partner, Josh, as he swung himself into the rescue helicopter waiting for them on the tarmac, its rotors already turning.

'I just won't do it and that's *that*.'

'Nice attitude, mate.' The chopper pilot, Steve, grinned at Tama. 'I'll just radio ahead and let the cops know so they can tell that poor blighter in the car that's rolled off the hill, shall I?'

'I'm not talking about the job.' Tama snapped his safety belt on.

Josh clicked his microphone into place. 'He's talking about whatever just went down in the station manager's office. You should've seen his face when he came out of that meeting.'

Steve requested clearance, got the helicopter airborne and quickly turned onto a flight path that would lead them to the accident site—their fifth and hopefully last callout for the day.

'What aren't you going to do, then?' he asked a couple of minutes later.

Tama made a growling sound that was magnified by the communication channel built into their helmets.

'Babysitting,' he said disgustedly.

'I don't get it.' Josh sounded puzzled. 'Weren't you having a meeting with the boss and Trev Elliot?'

'Sir Trevor?' Steve whistled. 'Doesn't he *own* the finance company that funds this rescue service?'

'Yes on both counts,' Tama responded gloomily.

'So what's that got to do with babysitting?'

'Sir Trevor has a *daughter*.' Tama made the word sound like an unfortunate encumbrance. 'One who's decided she likes the idea of joining our service.'

'And?'

'And we're not that far from Broken Hills.' Tama clicked the mouse on his laptop. 'I'll check the GPS co-ordinates for the incident.'

'Not required,' Steve told him. 'I can see beacons.' He banked the helicopter into another turn. 'Police, fire service and ambulance are already on site, they just can't bring the victim up from the vehicle.'

They circled over the scene. A car had left the road and lay, upside down, several hundred metres from any kind of level surface. It was good for the helicopter crew that there were no trees on the hillside but the car must have been travelling at a good speed by the time it had hit the rocky outcrop, which wasn't so good for the occupant. Emergency service personnel had scrambled down the hillside but it was obvious that conditions were tricky.

Tama pushed thought of Sir Trevor's daughter from his head.

'Definitely a winch job,' he announced. 'No way anyone could carry a stretcher up that hill.'

'And we're well over thirty minutes' drive from the nearest hospital.' Josh was also peering downwards as they hovered. 'Nappy or stretcher for the winch?'

'Let's find out.' Tama changed radio channels to put him in touch with the ground ambulance crew. 'Update on status and injuries?' he requested.

'Open fracture of the femur. Chest and abdo injuries.'

'Status?'

'Two. His breathing's painful, though. A few broken ribs at least. BP's down. Moderate blood loss—he wasn't found for a while. We've got fluids up, pain relief on board and a traction splint in place.'

'Excellent. We'll be with you asap.' He didn't need to confer with Josh to decide that a stretcher was necessary. It might be a lot quicker and easier to pick someone up with a nappy harness but this victim's injuries were too severe to make that an option.

Steve had widened his circle as Tama was talking. 'We can put down here and empty the back,' he said. 'The less weight the better with the way this wind's picking up.'

Emergency-vehicle beacons twinkled from a distance as the light faded and Steve put the helicopter down on a nearby hill. Tama and Josh worked swiftly to remove the fitted stretcher, seats and any equipment not needed for the initial stages of this rescue mission. The more weight on board, the higher the risk of being caught in a downdraft. Dropping a hundred feet or more when you had a patient on a stretcher and a crew member dangling from the aircraft would be a disaster.

The task completed, Tama checked his gear and winch harness and climbed into his new position in the back of the chopper, ready for Josh to winch him down to the accident scene. Thanks to treatment already given by paramedics, there was no need to ready the trauma pack for deployment.

'Ninety seconds,' Steve commended as they lifted off again. 'Not bad!'

Tama's quick glance and raised eyebrow at Josh was a shorthand 'thumbs-up' signal. They were a slick team all right, and a lot of that efficiency came from a combination of experience and physical strength.

Neither of which Trevor Elliot's daughter would possess.

The mental tug back to that extraordinary interview was not only annoying, it refused to get entirely banished and niggled away in the back of Tama's mind.

'Turning downwind,' Steve announced.

'Roger. Secure aft.' Josh had checked the winch was operational. He was ready for the job. More than ready. Tama could almost see an aura of adrenaline around his colleague.

'I have the target.' He glanced at Tama and, satisfied his crewmate was as ready as he was, he turned to the winch control panel. 'Checking winch power.'

On this final run, there shouldn't have been any time at all to think outside the protocol. He'd done this a hundred times or more. Stepping into an arctic blast of air. Bracing himself. Leaning out—knowing how much space there was between his back and the ground below.

'Clear skids,' Josh confirmed. 'Clear to boom out.'

'Clear.'

Tama relaxed into his harness as the weight was taken and he got lowered to just below the skids.

The lightweight stretcher between his legs obscured his vision of what lay below. For now, he was totally dependent on Josh and Steve for his position and safety.

His own adrenaline levels kicked up several notches. He turned inwards to summon the calm strength that never failed him. This was no job for anyone who couldn't face the fear and do it anyway.

He wouldn't go as far as to say it was no job for a woman but she'd have to be an exceptional specimen.

Trevor Elliot's daughter?

A princess whose bra size probably exceeded her IQ?

Not a snowball's chance in hell.

Dusk was a favourite time for fitness enthusiasts to hit the circuit built into the outskirts of Hagley Park in Christchurch.

Swinging from the rungs of a horizontal ladder—her feet well off the ground—was a slim woman with a determined expression on her face and curly blonde hair that was tied back in a ponytail damp with perspiration.

'Give it a break, Mikki.' A man stood to one side of the structure, bent forward, with his hands on his thighs as he tried to catch his breath. 'This is embarrassing.'

Mikki hung on the last rung for a moment. She grinned down at her running companion and then refocussed, sucking in a breath and then expelling it as she pulled her body upwards. Once…twice… The burn in muscles in her arms and shoulders increased to real pain. Once more for luck and then she dropped to the ground, bending her knees to cushion the impact.

'Ready, slug?'

The man groaned but caught up with Mikki's steady jog as she continued along the track, past runners going in the opposite direction, cyclists heading home from work and the slower obstacles of people walking their dogs.

'There's no stopping you, is there?'

Mikki had taken another detour a few minutes later, to use fat stumps of wood as stepping blocks.

'Not today, that's for sure. I'm so excited!'

'Yeah…I noticed.'

'We can do our stretches now.'

'Hallelujah!'

They shared the massive trunk of an ancient oak tree for support. Mikki bent one leg up behind her and held it to stretch her quads.

'I still can't believe it, John. They're going to let me have a go at joining air rescue. Choppers!'

'So you've said. More than once.' The admonition was tempered with a fond tone. 'Good luck. Not that you'll need it.'

'I don't know about that.' Mikki swapped to her other leg. 'The pre-requisite physical assessment is tough enough to wipe out well over half the people who apply and I've never even *heard* of a female that's made it through.'

'If anyone can, you can.' John was stretching his Achilles tendon now. 'Damn shame it means you have to shift north, though. We'll miss you.'

'I'll miss you guys, too, but this is…this is huge for me, John. This is what I've wanted ever since… Good grief, do you know I started dreaming about this when I was sixteen? Twelve years ago!' Mikki couldn't stop the grin spreading across her face. 'And I've made it. Isn't it *great*?'

'You really want to give up being an emergency department doctor to work as a paramedic? In helicopters?'

'I would have gone straight into the ambulance service instead of medical school, you know, but Dad wouldn't hear of it. He wasn't exactly happy when I told him I wanted to join Médecins Sans Frontières either. He's going to hit the roof when he finds out the kind of front-line training I'm going to do for the next few months.'

'Will he try to stop you?'

'I don't think so.' Mikki put a hand on her shoulder and pulled her elbow to extend the stretch. 'I reckon I've finally convinced him how important my career is to me. He can't wrap me in cotton wool for ever.'

'From what I've heard, your dad can do anything he likes. Hey, doesn't his company practically own air rescue services up north?'

'One of them funds the service, yes.' A frown appeared on Mikki's face. 'And I'll make sure that isn't public knowledge. I've earned the right to try out for this team. God knows, I've trained hard enough and applied often enough. If anyone suggests it's come from strings being pulled, I'll give them a black eye.'

John laughed. 'Yeah…right!'

'I'm serious.' Mikki straightened to her full height which was, unfortunately, only five feet two. 'I'm going to do this, John, and I'm going to do it all by myself. Just watch this space!'

* * *

The messroom of the air rescue base lay between the manager's office, where the walls were covered in maps and communication equipment occupied the space between desk and filing cabinets, and a hangar that housed two state-of-the-art, MBB-Kawasaki BK-117 helicopters. Referred to as simply 'the mess', its title was appropriate.

At one end of the large space was an entertainment area with a wide-screen television and comfortable armchairs big enough to sleep in. At the other end, a small kitchen provided facilities for snacks and meals. As usual, the bench space was cluttered with unwashed mugs, milk cartons that hadn't made it back to the fridge and leftover fast-food containers. The laminated surface of the dining table was virtually invisible thanks to the wealth of emergency medicine journals, memos, magazines and a well spread-out daily newspaper.

Two men were standing on the same side of the table, leaning forward as they perused the front page of the newspaper. A good third of that page was taken up with a photograph that could well win some photography award for the year.

Taken with a high-powered zoom lens from the roadside, the photographer seemed almost level with the chopper and virtually close enough to touch it. Steve was clearly intent on the control panel of the craft. Josh was perched in the side door with both feet on the lower skid, his safety harness pulled tight as he leaned out to take hold of the harness cradling the stretcher.

Tama's position was elegant. One hand held the pole at the rear of the side hatch, pushing his body and the stretcher holding their patient away from the skids as he positioned the burden. Josh was about to take hold of the head end of the stretcher to guide it into the back of the helicopter.

For some reason, Tama had glanced up as the photograph was taken. Maybe he had been checking the carabina linking the stretcher harness strop to the winch. His expression was serious enough to convey the drama of the moment.

It was also easily recognisable.

Josh dug his colleague in the ribs with his elbow. 'You're famous now, mate. The chicks will be queuing up.'

'Are you suggesting they don't already?'

Josh snorted but then grinned. 'At least it's put you in a better mood today.'

'Nah.' Tama straightened and turned towards the bench. 'I'm in a really bad mood, actually.'

'Why?'

'Apparently Princess Mikayla arrives today. Got any red carpet handy?' Tama opened a cupboard to reveal an empty shelf. With a grimace, he picked up a dirty mug and stepped to the sink.

'Why?' Josh repeated. 'We're not due for any prerequisite challenges for ages. Isn't four the minimum number of applicants before we even schedule a course?'

'This one's special.' Tama wrinkled his nose as he emptied long abandoned coffee down the plughole. He turned on the hot tap. 'I have to babysit from the get-go. Make sure she doesn't break a single, precious fingernail.'

'If she's worried about her nails, she won't get far with the pre-requisite.'

'No.' Tama searched for a teaspoon at the bottom of the sink and sounded far more cheerful. 'And that way, my friend, lies the light at the end of this tunnel.'

'You mean, she can't do the physical assessment until we get enough applicants?'

'Nah. I'm going to do it with her. I'll be the assessor *and* the competition.'

Josh looked thoughtful. 'You're not planning to make this assessment impossible to pass by any chance, are you?'

'Of course not.' Tama's expression was innocent. 'It's a tough enough call as it stands.'

'You're not kidding. The ten circuits of those steep grandstand stairs in less than ten minutes just about did me in.'

'Then there's the forty push-ups and forty sit-ups.'

'The hundred-metre swim and treading water for ten minutes.'

'And don't forget the twenty-kilo pack run.' Tama grinned at Josh. 'Hey, I'll just be doing my job. Won't be my problem if she's not up to scratch.'

Josh shook his head in warning. 'Don't go out of your way to put the boss's nose out of joint, will you? We'll all catch the flak if you do.'

Tama spooned coffee granules into his clean mug. 'The way I see it, I'll be saving us all a hell of a lot of time and trouble if her highness doesn't make the grade for any further training.'

Josh sighed. 'So what you're really saying is that you're planning to break her and dump her in one easy move.'

Tama merely raised his eyebrow with a 'neither confirm nor deny' expression. Then he turned on his most charming smile. 'Want a coffee, mate?'

The newspaper cutting was in the back pocket of a rather snug pair of jeans and knowing it was there was making Mikayla Elliot uncharacteristically flustered.

She hadn't expected to find that her assigned mentor was none other than the hero who had been splashed over the front page of today's paper.

The image had been impressive enough. That look of ferocious concentration combined with a calm confidence on the face of a man at the pinnacle of a career that had always been a fantasy job for Mikki. It was the whole image that had prompted her to cut the picture out like some starstruck teenager, however. The aircraft, the crew, the patient and—as a blurry backdrop—a wrecked vehicle in hostile terrain.

But it had only been one man's face that had been visible in the picture and that man was now standing right in front of her. As large as life.

No…larger. Tama James towered over Mikki by at least twelve inches and he was probably twice her body weight.

With no helmet, the slightly too long dark curls of his hair made a luxuriantly soft-looking frame for his face. The dark olive skin and almost black eyes suggested he was a good part Maori and that impression was heightened by the fact that he wasn't wearing overalls and just below the sleeve of his black T-shirt his upper arm was encircled by an ethnic tattoo that looked like a series of waves between intricate borders.

What would he think if he knew that a picture of himself was currently nestled against Mikki's right buttock?

The level of disdain she thought she could detect in those dark eyes would go through the roof, that's what.

'Sorry?' Wondering how secure that scrap of folded paper was in her pocket had actually made Mikki miss something Tama was saying.

His look remained level. His face deadpan. As though he had expected nothing less than an inability to concentrate from what he saw in front of him.

Mikki wished she had tied her shoulder-length hair back. Worn something a lot less figure-hugging than the jeans and top she had on beneath her jacket. She wished she was six inches taller and a good deal heavier.

Standing near Tama made her feel weirdly…fragile. Like a doll. Was it because of his size and the aura of power he exuded or was it simply a reflection of what *he* was seeing?

'I just asked about your level of fitness.'

'Oh…' Mikki cleared her throat. It wasn't easy to hold eye contact with this man but, dammit, she had to find and hang onto some self-confidence somehow. 'It's OK, I guess.'

'It'll need to be.' The other man in this incredibly messy boys' zone the station manager had brought her to was grinning. At least Josh was friendly. Or was he?

'The assessment's a bit of a killer,' he added. 'You might want to have a few days in the gym to get ready for it. You should probably—'

Tama quelled his partner's advice with just a look. 'My only free day off is tomorrow.' He turned his gaze back to Mikki. 'You up for it?'

Mikki stared back. She could see a gleam in his eyes and it wasn't the kind of gleam she was accustomed to seeing in the eyes of men. This was…smug, that's what it was.

He didn't think she had a chance of making the grade.

He thought she was wasting his time.

Any remnants of her smile faded.

'You bet,' she told Tama. 'Just tell me where and when.'

CHAPTER TWO

JUST a couple of hours. Maybe not sweet but at least short.

'Sorry. You certainly gave it your best shot and I have to say I'm a lot more impressed than I expected to be, but there's a good reason this pre-requisite is tough.'

Tama twisted the shower control and turned to eye his face in the bathroom mirror while the water heated up. Just as well he lived alone at the moment, the way he was talking aloud to himself like this.

Rehearsing.

He picked up a razor but then took a second glance in the mirror. A day's worth of stubble might not be a bad look for today. Rugged.

A man who cared about things more important than appearances.

A man who meant business.

Tama abandoned the razor, using the mirror to try and perfect a sympathetic smile that was less of a smirk.

'You can always try again some time. When you feel ready.'

The smile was quite genuine as he stepped into the

shower. It was well worth giving up half of one of his precious free days to rid himself of the irritating burden Princess Mikayla represented.

There was no smile on his face an hour later, however.

The vast sports stadium on the outskirts of the city had more than a few fitness freaks intent on an early workout but the areas Tama needed were deserted. Maybe that was why the appearance of Mikayla Elliot seemed dramatic.

He was sitting on one of the lower tiers of steep seating at one end of an Olympic-sized diving pool. Directly opposite the double doors that led to the women's changing area. Had she really needed to push both doors to announce her entrance?

And how could someone as tiny as this little princess appear to have such shapely legs? He'd noticed it yesterday in those tight jeans she'd been wearing. You'd think that Lycra bike shorts would have cut them off and made them look stumpy but, no…she may be small but she was perfectly proportioned.

At least the baggy T-shirt she had on right now was covering those intriguingly compact breasts that yesterday's top had accentuated. Sad, really. If he'd met this woman under any other circumstances he would have found her more than passably attractive, but anything other than a very brief professional encounter was definitely not on the cards. Tama doubted that Mikki would want to speak to him again after this morning.

His nod of approval was in recognition of the sensible trainers she had on her feet and the way she had scraped back that silly cloud of blonde curls that begged for a tiara rather than a flying helmet. Her hair was tight in a band high on the back of her head and the length had been tightly plaited.

Mikki's face looked just as pinched as she walked towards Tama with no hint of hesitation in her step. She dropped a bag on a seat below him, extracted a water bottle and towel and then smiled up at him, albeit a trifle grimly.

'OK. What's first?'

'See that staircase on the other side of these seats?' The almost vertical one. Big steps. Twenty of them.

'Yep.'

'You run up, along the front of the top row of seats and down the steps on the other side. Along the front by the pool and then up again.'

'Cool.' She was warming up. Bouncing slowly onto her toes and down again to wake up her Achilles tendons. Stretching her shoulders at the same time and taking deep breaths to pre-oxygenate herself. Looking disconcertingly ready to fire herself into the task like a bullet from a gun.

The enthusiasm might be commendable but it was irritating. Did she really think she could do this? Most guys, including Tama, found it a challenging workout. She'd last five circuits, tops.

'The goal is ten circuits in under ten minutes,' he told her.

She eyed a chunky sports watch she was wearing and pushed a button, presumably putting it into stopwatch mode. Then she eyed the grandstand, her gaze travelling as though memorising the route and assessing the timeframes needed.

She wasn't stupid, then. Anyone else might have earned a mental tick for being able to look at the big picture before tackling the first stage. In this case, Tama wasn't prepared to concede any points.

'Plus…' He eased himself to his feet. 'You're not doing it by yourself.'

'What?' The plait on the back of Mikki's head swung as she looked over her shoulder. 'Someone else is coming?'

'No.'

Dammit! The way she stayed silent in the face of confusion, a tiny frown puckering her forehead as she waited for clarification, was also commendable. She wasn't about to jump to erroneous conclusions. And that look would extract the necessary information from anyone. There was an air of authority about this pint-sized princess. She was used to ruling her subjects. Tama hid a grin. He wasn't one of them.

'I'm doing it with you.' He stripped off the hooded jacket he was wearing. He knew the black singlet top did nothing to conceal the kind of physical condition he kept himself in but intimidation was a legitimate tool, wasn't it? He owed it to any candidate to make sure they gave their best performance.

The flicker he saw in Mikki's eyes as they widened was certainly gratifying.

'I thought you were doing the assessment.'

'Correct.' Tama deliberately flexed his upper body muscles in a slow stretch. 'It's quite possible to do both.'

'Right.'

She looked disconcerted. Used to being the focus of attention rather than a team member? A mental cross this time instead of a tick. Good. Tama held her gaze.

'Normally we don't run an assessment unless we've got at least four people ready to try out for the team.'

'So why am I doing it by myself?'

Tama's smile was one-sided. 'I guess you're special.' He twisted his body, elbows raised, partly to stretch but more to avoid eye contact. It would be unprofessional to mention her father and strings being pulled and, besides, if he got started, he might go too far. Might tell her what it was like to be one of twelve children—included but never really belonging. Fighting for any of the good things life had to offer. Struggling to get the kind of chances people like her had handed to them on silver platters.

A careful breath and he was under control. 'It helps to have someone else sharing the suffering,' he said more lightly. 'And it can make a difference, having a bit of competition. We're often pushed to or even beyond physical limits in this job.'

A single nod. 'You've done this before, of course.'

'Many times.' Tama conceded the advantage. 'But this is an initial evaluation, not a race. I don't expect you to have the kind of fitness level we maintain once we're in the job.' He didn't expect her to have much at all, did he?

She hadn't broken the eye contact. 'And you've been in the job how long?'

'Coming up to ten years.'

'And you do this kind of training how often?'

'We get reassessed every six months.'

She finally looked away, towards the cliff face of concrete steps. Then she stripped off the T-shirt to reveal a singlet top that clung just as tightly as Tama's did. He had to drag his eyes away from the faint outline of her ribs and the firm, perfect curves of her breasts. The size of good oranges, he decided.

Nice. His gaze flicked back involuntarily as he caught the movement a deep breath engendered. Fortunately, Mikki didn't notice his line of vision. She was looking at the steps.

'Ready when you are.'

If anything was going to kill her, this was.

The first five circuits had been OK. No more daunting that her usual park sessions, really, but then the punishing regime began to bite.

At least the man beside her was panting as hard as she was and his face was set in fierce lines of concentration.

Six circuits. Seven. Mikki knew she was slowing down but a glance at her stopwatch showed she had four minutes left. She dug deep. Visualised herself wearing the bright orange overalls of a helicopter crew member. Told herself they were climbing a mountain to get to a seriously injured patient.

Eight circuits. Nine. It hurt to suck in a breath now and she would probably be able to collect several hundred mils of fluid if she wrung out her hair and clothing. A sheen of sweat glistened on the rippling muscles ahead of her. Mikki watched the bulge of Tama's quads as he climbed step after step. She tried to force her own legs to match his rhythm.

She came very close to calling it quits on the upward leg of the last circuit. Halfway up and each step was so hard all Mikki wanted to do was melt into a puddle of overextended body parts. Preferably lose consciousness until life seemed worth living once more.

Just a few more steps, she reminded herself fuzzily. Then the straight bit and down the other side and you've made it. *He'll* be watching. He'll be impressed.

And that was enough to be able to do what seemed impossible. To keep pushing. To arrive at the end of this first test only a few seconds behind her assessor.

Did it matter that she flopped to the ground to sit on her bottom with her knees raised, her arms crossed on top of them and her head using them as a pillow? It must have been nearly a minute before Mikki had recovered enough for the roaring in her head to cease and she could raise it to see the expression on Tama's face.

Admiration.

Grudging maybe, but unmistakable.

Yes!

Mikki managed a smile. 'What's next, then?'

He actually grinned. 'No stopping you, is there, princess?'

It was a big ask to catch totally inadequate breath and glare at the same time but Mikki gave it a good shot.

'Princess?'

He had the grace to look…what, guilty? How odd.

'I work with blokes. We're into nicknames.'

Mikki digested the comment. He didn't want a woman on the team—was that what he had against her? Fair enough. She could overcome that kind of prejudice if she was given the opportunity.

'What's yours, then?'

'My what?'

'Nickname.'

'Don't have one.' Tama raised his face from the towel he was holding and frowned. 'Actually, I'd never noticed. I'm just me, I guess.'

Yeah…

Mikki copied his example, mopping perspiration from her face and neck. Drinking water and flexing muscles ready for the next challenge. Her gaze kept straying, however. Peeking. Taking in the fairly well-exposed and absolutely ripped body of her companion. His height and the width of his shoulders. Good grief, Tama James could probably pick her up with one hand and tuck her under his arm.

And why did that thought create an odd ache that had absolutely nothing to do with the strenuous physical activity her body had just been subjected to?

OK, he was attractive.

More than attractive. His face, with such strong features and eyes as dark as sin, would have made any female take a second glance. Factor in the 'just got out of bed' stubble, that glorious olive skin and that tattoo and you got a package that was so far out of any realm Mikki had experienced it was hardly surprising she was intrigued.

Plus, he was a hero in her dream career. Top of the ladder. There was automatic respect and admiration in place.

'You're staring.' The tone was accusing.

'Sorry.' At least her face was probably red enough to cover a blush. 'I've never worked with anyone who has, um, a tattoo like yours, that's all.'

'You're not working with me,' Tama said coolly. 'Yet. You ready for the next bit?'

'You mean I passed the last one?' The reminder that she couldn't consider herself a colleague needled Mikki. She couldn't resist making him remember how she'd kept up with his own efforts. Or had he slowed down for her benefit?

He was avoiding her gaze. 'All good so far,' he said calmly. 'Heaps to get through yet, though.'

Mikki smiled. 'Bring it on.'

Dammit, but this small, blonde bombshell was like the bloody battery bunny. She just went on and on. Through the press-ups and the sit-ups that Tama did at a speed that made his whole body burn. She seemed to enjoy the cooling-off the hundred-metre swim provided and treading water for ten minutes looked like a rest period.

If he couldn't crack her with the pack run, there was no way out of this babysitting lark.

Curiously, the notion of sending the princess packing was not nearly as appealing as it had been first thing this morning.

'Tell me why,' Tama ordered as he handed her the small backpack with a twenty-kilogram weight inside. 'Why do you want to join a helicopter team?'

'Preparation. I want to add the skills to my CV.'

'To what end?'

'MSF. Mèdecins San Frontiéres.'

'I know what it is.' Tama shook the incredulous expression from his face. 'I've thought about it myself.' He slid his arms through his pack straps. 'You're talking global hotspots. Third-world conditions. *War* zones.'

'Think I'm not up to it?'

Man, there was a bit of fire in there! Tama liked that. Sparks kept things hot.

'Didn't say that. Just curious as to why you'd want to.'

'Maybe I'm an adrenaline junkie.'

'*Are* you?' Thrill seekers who might take unnecessary risks and endanger other team members were not welcome on Tama's watch.

Mikki shook her head dismissively. 'I know the value of staying alive, if that's what you're getting at. I was in a major car crash when I was sixteen. Got a good look at what it would be like not to survive and I don't plan on repeating the experience.'

Tama nodded acknowledgement. He was tempted to ask more but that would be hardly professional, would it? He had no excuse to stray onto personal ground.

Yet.

'Having said that,' Mikki continued, 'I'm not exactly a shrinking violet either, and when I heard that MSF were short of doctors, I put my hand up.'

Tama's thoughts had been veering towards sympathy for Sir Trevor Elliot who probably had good reason to be concerned about his daughter's safety. They slammed to a halt.

'You're a *doctor*?'

'What did you think I was?'

Tama's mouth opened and then closed. Opened again. Preconceptions were exploding somewhere in the back of his mind, pretty dresses and low IQs among them. 'They…ah…said you worked in an emergency department, that's all. I…ah…'

'Assumed I was a nurse? A phlebotomist? Desk clerk?' Mikki gave an incredulous huff and turned away. 'Let's get this over with, shall we? I've got a manicure booked for later today.'

* * *

She had to reach out and touch it just to convince herself it was real and not part of a dream.

It was hanging at the end of a row of hooks. A bright orange set of long-sleeved overalls with horizontal fluorescent strips below the elbows and knees and the official air rescue insignia on the front.

'Had to be specially ordered in,' Josh told her. 'Smallest size they've ever been asked for.'

'They were quick. It's only been three days since I passed the pre-requisite.' Mikki stole a glance at the lead member of her mentor crew but Tama was looking at his partner.

'What was it they asked? If we had a mouse joining the crew?'

'Hey…Mickey Mouse!'

Oh…no! Surely that awful nickname that she thought she'd left behind at primary school wasn't about to resurface?

'Mouse,' Tama echoed thoughtfully. 'Hmm. Small and very…'

Mikki gave him a look. If he dared suggest she was scared of anything, he was going to regret it.

His lips curved. For the first time Mikki saw genuine amusement in his face and it came alive, with sparks of real mischief in the dark depths of his eyes. And, boy, he knew exactly what he was doing here. Did he have the intelligence to recognise limits?

'And smart,' he said innocently. 'Perfect.' His smile took on a wicked edge that warned Mikki he wasn't conceding victory quite yet. She followed his gaze as it travelled to where her hand was unconsciously stroking the fabric of her shiny new overalls.

'Just like your nails,' he added. 'Good job.'

Mikki drew in a breath. Some limits might need neon signs.

'Just for the record,' she informed him, 'I do not get manicures. My hair colour is natural and I have no intention of ever getting a boob job. Satisfied?'

His eyes widened a fraction but there was a flash of something other than feigned submission as he held his hands up, palms outward. Either he approved of her standing up for herself or he thought there was nothing wrong with the size of her breasts.

Mikki looked away. Tama might not be satisfied but *she* was. Enough to call a private truce. She'd let them get away with calling her 'Mouse' if that's what it took to join this team.

It still seemed like a dream but those overalls were real. She bit back a grin as she finally stopped touching them. It should be enough that she was wearing the black pants and T-shirt with the base insignia. That she had the heavy black boots with steel-capped toes on her feet already.

'What happens today?' Mikki queried.

'Depends,' Tama responded unhelpfully.

'On?'

'Callouts,' Josh supplied. He gave his partner an unreadable look but Mikki suspected a friendly reprimand was included. 'If it's quiet, Tama's going to start your basic training.'

'Cool.'

'Yeah.' Tama didn't seem to be sharing her enthusiasm, however. 'There's a lot to get through.'

'Such as?'

'Procedures. How to use the paging system. Map reading. Basic chopper safety. Gear…'

Josh groaned. 'Speaking of gear, I've got to get on with the stockroom check and clean up. It's a mess thanks to how busy we've been. Want to swap, Tama? I could train Mouse.'

Mikki's gaze flew to catch Tama's.

Those undercurrents in her pre-requisite assessment had been unmistakable. He hadn't thought she was a suitable candidate. He'd almost given the impression of experiencing physical pain when he'd had to tell her she'd passed and would be allowed to join the team for further training.

And then he'd gone. Just turned on his heel and left. It had been the station manager, Andy, who'd called her later to congratulate her and provide the information needed for the next stage, which had included arrangements for her uniform and other necessities.

Now Tama had the opportunity to step back. To give away the mentorship he'd been assigned. Was it permissible? Would he want to? Her gaze remained riveted on Tama's and it was the paramedic who finally broke the eye contact.

'Nah,' he drawled. Had the decision been a close call? 'I hate that paperwork that goes with a stocktake. I'll keep the mouse.'

Mikki had to stop an outward rush of breath. Had she been holding it? Why?

Because Tama was the senior crew member here, in every way, that's why. Josh was a nice guy and probably extremely competent but Tama's aura of confidence and ability and sheer…*power* was palpable.

This was the man Mikki wanted to work with despite whatever he might think of her.

And she wanted to work with him as closely as possible.

CHAPTER THREE

HE SHOULD have been more careful about what he wished for.

Things had started well enough. After a brief tour of the base, issuing Mikki with a pager and explaining how it worked, Tama had taken her into the hangar. One of the helicopters was already outside, with Steve busy checking it, which left plenty of space for them to stand back and admire the back-up aircraft.

'New Zealand was the first place in the world where a helicopter was used for rescue work, back in 1970.'

'Really?' Mikki stepped closer. 'I didn't know that.'

'It was only used for beach rescues for a long time. It wasn't till 1983 that we started to use them for general rescues.'

Mikki nodded. She seemed to be soaking up the information and Tama found himself unexpectedly enjoying his role. He dismissed the reaction and took a quick glance at his watch. And that was when he started wishing that his pager would go off and give him an excuse to escape Mikki's company for a while.

'It's got an eight- to twelve-seat capacity if it's not

used for medical evacuation but our stretchers and gear take up a lot of seating room. We're set up to carry seven people and a stretcher or four people and two stretchers.'

'What's the range?'

'Five-forty kilometres, depending on weight and weather and so on. We've got auxiliary tanks that extend that quite a bit. Its maximum speed is 278 kilometres an hour and it has a ceiling of ten thousand feet.' She wasn't really interested in the chopper's technical data, was she?

'So how far can we go on a job?'

'We'. It still rankled that she was here. That Tama would have to spend so much time and effort allowing her to gain a qualification that she intended to take elsewhere. If she wasn't Trevor Elliot's daughter, this would not be a happening thing, would it? And 'we' would not be going on any jobs for as long as Tama could keep a lid on this situation. He'd like to go on one, though, right about now. It wasn't going to stay this quiet all day, was it?

'Operations are normally kept within a 160-kilometre range of base, allowing forty-five minutes each way for travelling and thirty minutes at the rescue scene.'

Tama cleared his throat. He needed to get on with the training tasks assigned for the day. If it was going to stay quiet, then the sooner they got through them, the sooner he could get on with the backlog of journals he wanted to catch up on in his downtime.

'How much do you know about helicopter safety?'

'A bit. I worked in the ED of a hospital that had a helipad on the roof. I know not to approach or leave without pilot clearance and to stay in his line of vision.

And not to go near when the engine is starting up or running down because the rotors change height.'

'There's a few other considerations when we're out in the field. If you get blinded by dust or something, you have to stop and crouch or sit down. One of us will assist you. If you're carrying any gear, keep it horizontal and below waist level.'

They moved to the rear of the helicopter where the clamshell doors were open.

Mikki looked impressed. 'There's a lot of gear in there.'

'We've got a full set of what you'd expect in a well-equipped ambulance. Full resus gear, including 12-lead ECG monitoring, defibrillator with pacing capability. Suction, traction splints, scoop stretcher, IV gear, fluids, drugs. Usual stuff. Everything we need for initial stabilisation is in this kit.' Tama touched the large, soft pack strapped near the back of the machine against a folded scoop stretcher and the lightweight stretcher used for winching. 'Come and meet our pilot, Steve. He should be finished whatever he's doing outside now.'

He was. And he seemed delighted to meet Mikki. Proud to show off his sleek aircraft.

'Jump in,' he invited. 'See what it feels like from the inside. Ever been up in one of these?'

'No. Lots of small planes but never a chopper.'

Small planes. Tama almost snorted. Gulfstream jets more likely.

'I've got my private pilot's licence,' Mikki added casually, as she climbed into the copilot's seat. 'And I've done a bit of gliding.'

'Phew! You'll be flying one of these yourself next.'

Steve's gaze was openly admiring and it irritated the hell out of Tama.

'I'll do that,' he growled, moving past Steve before he could show Mikki how the safety belts worked. 'Don't let us interrupt your pre-flight stuff. We could get a job any minute, eh?'

He wished! It just wasn't comfortable having this woman within the close confines of a helicopter, which became more noticeable when they moved into the back so she could see the various seating options and how all the gear fitted. Unbearably so when Tama helped Mikki put on and adjust a seating harness.

It was inevitable that he was close enough to discover that her hair smelt of…what, strawberries? Something summery and fresh, anyway. As fresh as the puff of her breath he could feel on his neck as he leaned in. And there was no way he could avoid brushing her body with his hands on more than one occasion.

This was why he didn't like the idea of having a female crew member. It was distracting.

Alarmingly so, in this case. She didn't simply have the usual kind of feminine attractions that any man was programmed to take notice of, she had kept up with him under gruelling physical challenges that would have destroyed a lot of men. She was intelligent. And she had a pilot's licence as well? *Sheesh!*

Why wouldn't that damn pager go off? Tama wished harder and his wish came true. The pager beeped stridently and when Mikki had silenced hers, she looked up at Tama and her face was glowing.

'A job!' Her gaze held a plea that would have melted virtually any man. 'Will I be able to come, too?'

'No,' Tama snapped as he read the message on the pager. That was not part of the wish.

'Why not?' It wasn't Mikki asking. Steve walked past the open hatch on his way to the pilot's seat. 'We've got the room.'

Tama quelled him with a look that warned his colleague not to interfere. 'It might be a winch job,' he informed Mikki. 'You've had no training and you'd just get in the way. We'd end up dumping you in a paddock somewhere, along with all the other non-essential weight.'

The excitement drained from her face and a hint of colour crept into her cheeks. Mikki dropped her gaze instantly, presumably thinking she could disguise her disappointment, and her tone was light as she unclipped the harness.

'That's cool. There's plenty I can do here, I expect.'

Dammit. Did she have to be so reasonable? Tama strode into the mess room to pull on his overalls. Josh was a step ahead of him.

'Just a prang,' he told Tama. 'Roadside. Easy landing.'

'No winching, then?' Mikki was watching Josh but Tama saw the way her gaze slid towards the peg that her own overalls were hanging on.

'Not this time.'

Now Tama could feel Mikki's gaze on him. A silent query this time but one that would need a different explanation to cover his refusal. He could come up with several.

Like not knowing where gear was, for example, when it might be needed in a hurry. Say…a suction kit. Having to take the time to make sure she was following protocols regarding crew safety when his attention would be better spent on the patient. She might argue, of course, but that would be good. He'd rather see her angry than disappointed. He doubted very much that he would see any expression of defeat, however.

Did he want to?

Yes. No.

This was confusing. Having Mikki here was distracting *and* confusing and Tama didn't like it one little bit. The only saving grace was that it was temporary. And the sooner she got her damned qualification, the sooner she would be out of his place of work *and* his life.

She was still staring at him.

'Fine.' Tama kept his gaze on the zip he was pulling closed. 'You can come. But you'll have to do exactly what you're told, *when* you're told. Got it?'

'Got it.' Mikki was already halfway into her overalls. 'Hey, Tama?'

'What?' Both the tone and the eye contact were reluctant.

Her smile was almost shy. 'Thanks.'

His only response was a grunt as he jammed his helmet over his head. What was it about this princess? How could just a smile—and not even a real one at that—stir some odd sensation in his gut?

He couldn't identify the sensation but it made him feel…bigger somehow. Important. Powerful, even.

Confusing, that's what it was all right.

And Tama James did not like feeling confused.

This was *so* exciting!

Mikki would have hugged herself with the sheer thrill of it all but imagine if Tama saw that? He'd already caught her stroking her new overalls like some dreamy bride mooning over her confection of a frock.

She kept herself very, very still in her seat, thankful no one could see what was happening inside. The way her heart lifted to her mouth to mirror the helicopter rising into the air and then beat a tattoo against her ribs as they took off into a clear, blue sky. The way her stomach swooped and clenched when they hit some turbulence.

Don't be sick, she begged silently. *Please!*

'You all right?' Tama was giving her a suspicious look. Had he guessed her inner turmoil and the very real possibility that her stomach might not cope?

'I'm good,' Mikki assured him. And she was. She *had* to be!

'It's about a twenty-minute ride,' Tama said, still watching her. 'There's two vehicles involved and the fire service is only arriving on scene now so we might arrive to find people still trapped.'

Mikki nodded. Her head felt heavy with the unfamiliar helmet and her nod was probably over-eager. She became still again. This was her first opportunity to show Tama what she was capable of professionally and she was determined not to mess it up.

'Take a look around in the back here.'

They had their helmet radios on a different channel to the one Josh and Steve were using as they discussed navigation. Tama's voice, inside the helmet, was so clear and close it was disturbingly intimate. As though he had his mouth right beside her ear, his lips close enough to touch her skin.

And that gave Mikki a shiver to add to the strange physical sensations this ride was already clocking up.

'We haven't had a chance to go through the gear in here.' Tama's voice continued to caress her ear. 'Might be a good idea if you at least knew where the basics were.'

She was ready for the weight of the helmet this time. Her nod was carefully controlled.

'You can talk, you know,' Tama said drily. 'You've got a mike as well as earphones in there.'

'OK.'

'See where the portable oxygen is?'

'Yes.'

'There's adult and child masks, acute and nebuliser, plus a non-rebreather in the pouch.'

'What's in that big pack?'

'It's called a Thomas pack. It's got pretty well everything and it's what we take from the chopper for a job like this. Blood-pressure cuffs and a stethoscope, chest decompression sets, intubation gear, bag mask unit, IV gear, fluids and drugs. We'll go through it properly when we're back at base.'

Mikki had a sudden inkling of what this was like from Tama's viewpoint. She was being allowed out on a job before she really had any idea about resources and protocols. Before he had any idea what her level of skill was. He was probably thinking—quite rightly—that she could be a hindrance rather than any help.

Mikki took a deep breath and tried to quell her rush of nerves but they came back with a vengeance when they slowly circled the scene and came in to land. The view from up high was spectacular but getting the big picture with such clarity made this all seem almost overwhelming.

Traffic was backed up for miles in both directions,

with police cars blocking the road well away from the accident site, so that even before Mikki could glimpse what they were heading for, she already had the impression it was major.

More police cars. Fire engines and two ambulances and so many people made up the inner circle and there—in its centre—were two horribly mangled vehicles. A car and a small truck. Mikki could see someone lying on the ground and another sitting with ambulance officers in attendance. And, judging by the cluster of rescue workers, someone else was still trapped in the car.

Multiple patients, potentially critically injured, but it shouldn't be throwing her into this kind of a spin. She dealt with the aftermath of MVAs all the time in Emergency and she was good at it. They often had more than one victim arrive from a single incident.

But this was very, very different.

These people hadn't already been triaged and stabilised by competent paramedics. Removed from a scene of carnage to arrive neatly packaged on a stretcher into a department that was well prepared with equipment and personnel. This was frontline stuff with an emotional element Mikki hadn't expected, thanks to seeing the lines of traffic and the scope of the rescue effort and being there—in real time—to imagine the shock of having one's life so unexpectedly thrown into chaos.

You know what to do, Mikki reminded herself as the helicopter touched down in a paddock beside the road, far enough away for the rotor wash not to create havoc. It's basic. Airway, breathing, circulation. Assess each one and deal with it if it's not adequate before moving on to the next. It may be more difficult and messier out here in the field but the priorities were the same.

And this was exactly where she wanted to be, wasn't it? Frontline. Dealing with all the complications any kind of environment could create. Relying on her own skills and resources that would be far less than those an emergency department could offer. She wasn't being thrown into this alone, in any case. She was with someone who was the top of their field. She was here to learn.

Confidence was available after all. She had Tama by her side. Mikki gathered all she could find as she followed him towards the car. Josh peeled off, after a brief, almost non-verbal communication with his senior partner, to go to the ambulance officers attending the people already out of the vehicles. Two more ambulance officers were right beside the car. The rear door had been cut away and a woman perched on the back seat, holding the driver's head in a position that would keep his airway open and protect his neck.

Another straightened from where the front door had also been cut away.

'He's unresponsive,' the paramedic informed Tama. 'They've only just pulled the truck clear and got these doors off for us so I haven't even completed my assessment, sorry.'

Tama leaned in. 'Hey, mate,' he called. 'Can you hear me? Can you open your eyes?' His fingers were on the man's wrist, and then his neck. 'Carotid pulse,' he said aloud. 'No radial. BP's well down.'

'He's bleeding heavily,' the paramedic noted. 'His leg's trapped under the dash.'

A fireman moved in from the crumpled bonnet of the

car. 'We're about to do a dash roll. You'll be able to get him out then.'

Mikki had to move as a thick hose was pulled past her feet, a piece of equipment attached to its end that looked like a modified pneumatic drill. She was trying to concentrate on the continuing communication be-tween Tama and the road-based paramedic but this was no emergency department handover.

The pneumatic gear the fire service were using was loud enough to mean people had to shout to communi-cate and everyone seemed to have urgent tasks that other people were being ordered to carry out. The woman on the ground a short distance away was screaming and a new, approaching siren added to the cacophony.

It smelt of hot metal and petrol and blood and every-thing looked deformed and sharp. Dangerous.

'Can you move?' A fireman requested curtly. He was holding the heavy-looking cutting gear. 'I need to get in here.'

'Give us a minute,' Tama ordered. 'I want to get an IV in and some oxygen on before we do anything more.' He slid the Thomas pack off his back and, magically, enough clear space opened beside him to allow the pack to be opened out. 'Mikki? You want to get the IV in?'

'Sure.'

She hoped she sounded sure. An eagerness to show Tama what she could do—*please* him, even—bubbled inside her, and he'd handed her what should be an easy way to begin. Apart from having to step around the crumpled driver's door on the ground, access wasn't a problem. The paramedic unhooked a pair of shears from his belt and cut through the jersey and shirt covering her patient's arm. Mikki slid a tourniquet on and pulled it tight.

Tama leaned past to slip an oxygen mask over the man's face, then he hooked the stethoscope hanging around his neck into his ears and leaned in to listen to the man's chest. The paramedic was waiting his turn to get close, a stiff neck collar in his hands.

'Chest and neck injuries,' Tama informed Mikki succinctly. 'I'm not happy with his airway but an OP will have to do until we get him out. BP's well down so I want to get fluids started stat.'

Mikki just nodded, concentrating on gaining access to a forearm vein with the wide-bore cannula she held. It wasn't easy. Their patient was a very large man and she was having to go on touch rather than a visual target. To her relief, blood flowed into the chamber instantly. She advanced the needle a little further, slid the cannula home and withdrew the mechanism.

'Got a luer plug?'

'Here.' The paramedic had a dressing and tape ready to secure the line as well and then a giving set and bag of fluids appeared with commendable swiftness, but if Mikki had expected any praise for succeeding in her task, she would have been disappointed. Not that there was time to think of it because things were moving very rapidly now.

Josh joined them.

'Truck driver's only got minor injuries and the female passenger from the car is stable. They're both being transported by road. Where are we here?'

They were at the point of being able to move their patient. Mikki stood back, letting the more experienced and stronger men put on an impressive display of peeling back crumpled metal and then using a body splint and backboard to turn and slide the victim free with minimal disruption to his spinal alignment.

The unconscious driver was on a stretcher within a very short period of time, moved clear of the wreckage, but securing him in the helicopter was still some way off, it appeared. The man's breathing was deteriorating and Tama clearly wanted to try and stabilise his condition prior to transport. He opened pockets of the Thomas pack and took out a large, tightly rolled package.

Mikki was using the stethoscope as Tama untied the package and opened it up to reveal an intubation kit. She nodded her agreement.

'He's got some bleeding going on in his trachea,' she said. 'And I don't like this swelling in his neck. If we don't secure his airway now, we might lose it completely.'

'Absolutely.' Tama was holding up a pair of gloves that looked far too small for his hands. 'Go for it, Doc.'

Mikki couldn't help her jaw dropping in astonishment.

Technically, she had higher qualifications than either of the paramedic air rescue crew. She had intubated dozens of people in emergency departments and Theatre but these guys had the huge advantage of experience in working under precisely these conditions.

Rescue crews were still busy around them. It was noisy and dirty and…foreign. And this was an obese patient who could be difficult to intubate even under ideal circumstances. Tama was throwing her in the deep end here but she had breezed through that cannulation, hadn't she?

She could do this, too.

Except it was harder than she had feared. With blood

in the airway and bright sunlight negating the effect of the laryngoscope's light, it was impossible.

'I can't see a thing,' Mikki had to admit.

'Here. I'll shade you.' Tama loomed close over Mikki and the man's head, blocking the light from falling directly on them.

Mikki still couldn't visualise the vocal cords. It was hard to keep a note of desperation from her voice.

'I need suction.'

'It's here.' Tama managed to slip the handle of the suction unit inside their patient's mouth without dislodging the laryngoscope Mikki held in place. She reached for an ET tube.

'Here goes,' she muttered hopefully.

Her first attempt failed.

'Oxygen saturation is dropping.' Josh was right beside her. 'I'll bag mask him for a sec.'

Mikki sat back on her heels, looking for a replacement tube in the kit. She caught Tama's steady gaze. 'Maybe you should do this,' she suggested. Or Josh could. Except that Josh was now responding to a signal from a fire officer. It looked as though one of the rescue workers had injured himself.

'Have another go,' Tama directed.

So she did and again it proved impossible.

'The trachea's swelling,' she said in despair. 'I can't get this past the cords even with a guide wire.'

'I'll have a go.'

They swapped places. Tama handed her the bag-mask unit and she held the mask over the man's face, squeezing the bag to try and get a high concentration of oxygen into the man's lungs. She could feel it becoming more difficult as the airway closed further. Tama was pulling on gloves. As he picked up the laryngoscope, Mikki could hear the deterioration in the man's breathing. A nasty stridor that suggested they might be about to lose this challenge.

Tama positioned himself and the patient's head. He inserted the laryngoscope.

'Give me some cricoid pressure,' he instructed seconds later.

Mikki pressed on an Adam's apple that was actually hard to locate in an already thick neck that had severe swelling going on as well. If things were this hard from the outside, what hope did Tama have of slipping a tube through the airway internally?

Very little, but he managed. Almost instantly, he slipped the tube into place and then straightened to secure it and attach the bag mask to the end of the tube. Mikki picked up the unit as Tama placed his stethoscope on the chest. She squeezed the bag as he listened for lung sounds and then placed the disc below the ribs to exclude air going into the epigastrium.

'We're in,' he announced calmly. 'Let's get this guy on board and get moving.'

The packing up and preparation for take off were practised and smooth. Josh returned and again Mikki was left on the outskirts of the routine, simply watching.

No wonder. She had messed up, hadn't she? Failed on the first real medical challenge that had been thrown her way.

She was a liability. Tama hadn't wanted her on his crew in the first place and now he had good reason to resent her inclusion.

No wonder he was so focussed on his patient he didn't spare her even a glance on the homeward journey. No surprise she wasn't asked to assist in any medical capacity either. These guys had it sorted. Intensive monitoring, another IV line, fluids going in under pressure, a badly broken leg dressed and splinted.

She was just a passenger. An unwanted one. Present but not included, and it stirred memories Mikki had thought long buried.

They came in to land on the hospital helipad with their patient still stable and breathing well. The two paramedics were clearly satisfied with the way the job had gone. Tama seemed to have forgotten the debacle with intubation but Mikki couldn't. She had to bite her lip and blink away a very unexpected prickle in her eyes that suggested the possibility of tears.

She was about to *cry*?

No way!

Mikki clenched her jaw tight as she climbed out of the helicopter to follow the stretcher. She wasn't going to let it matter that Tama didn't want her. That she had played into his hands by begging to go on a job and then demonstrating a very uncharacteristic lack of ability.

He'd give her another chance.

He *had* to.

CHAPTER FOUR

'HAPPY?'

'Yeah…sure,' Tama replied.

Josh quirked an eyebrow. 'You should be. You don't have to carry on with the incredibly boring stocktake.'

This was true. If it remained quiet on station he could carry on with Mikki's training. She needed to learn how to load and unload the stretchers. How to secure sliding doors and all the medical gear and what to check before telling the pilot that 'all was secure in the rear'.

'Do you know how many individual components we have in IV gear alone?'

'No.' And Tama didn't know why he wasn't as happy as he claimed to be either.

'Fourteen,' Josh said in disgust. 'Five different gauges of cannula, wipes, luer plugs, giving sets, Tegaderm, tape…'

Tama pushed open the door of the men's changing room, barely registering the list. Mikki wasn't in the kitchen end of the messroom and it was well past time they had some lunch. Where was she?

'Then there's four sizes of syringes and six sizes of

needles on top of that,' Josh continued, 'and I have to count every single one of them.' He, too, looked around the room. 'Where's the mouse?'

'Dunno.'

'She was kind of quiet when we got to the hospital. If the job had been a bit much for her, I would have expected her to feel happy to be on familiar turf, even if it wasn't an ED she's worked in. She didn't look happy, though, did she?'

'No.'

'Maybe she doesn't like it as much as she thought she would. She looked pretty excited when we headed off.'

'Yeah.' That glow had been well and truly snuffed out, hadn't it? And Tama knew why. Having been called to check that fire officer, Josh hadn't seen Tama take over the intubation of that difficult patient. He had no idea how tense it had been. How lucky Tama had been to succeed on his first try and how it must have made Mikki feel like she'd messed up and shown herself to be less than competent.

The wind had been taken out of the royal sails all right. Tama had demonstrated his own prowess at her expense. He should be pleased with himself. Experiencing the kind of satisfaction that had once been a dream—to prove that someone like him was just as good, if not better, than someone like her. He should be *happy*, dammit!

'Coffee?'

'Sure.' Maybe she was still in the tiny bathroom area kept for visitors that was now deemed the female locker room. That would be it. She probably needed to touch up her mascara or nail polish or something after working rough.

I don't do manicures.

Josh turned from where he was fossicking in the fridge. 'And how about I nuke the leftover chow mein we put in the freezer last week?'

Tama nodded. He wasn't bothered about what they ate. He was more bothered by how clearly he could hear Mikki's words echoing in his head. She wasn't into nail polish. Her hair colour was natural and she liked the size of her breasts. So *there*!

Tama could feel a corner of his mouth pulling sideways. Spirit like that was something he could approve of. Like the way she had punished herself keeping up with him during those pre-requisite challenges. She had been so determined to make the grade, hadn't she? To prove she was up to the job.

Had that spirit been snuffed out, along with the glow?

OK, the glow had been irritating but that was partly because he understood it. Not that he'd ever let it show on *his* face like that. At least, he hoped he hadn't, but he knew what it was like to get a shot at something you wanted badly enough to get so excited about. And he also knew what it was like to want something that badly and have it all turn to custard. To blame yourself for whatever was going wrong. He hoped Mikki wasn't into beating herself up too thoroughly. While it might be good to have tarnished the glow a little, crushing that spirit entirely would not only be unnecessary, it could lead to repercussions. What if the boss learned that the princess was unhappy? Who would be held accountable? Him, that's who.

Josh was pushing buttons on the microwave and Tama should have been looking forward to the food, not standing here, worrying about the mental state of an extra crew member.

The faint growling sound he emitted did not come from his empty stomach.

Josh looked over his shoulder. 'What's up?'

'Just need a bit a fresh air. Be back in a minute. Don't eat it all.'

Patting his pocket as he strode through the hangar on his way outside was automatic. Remembering that he'd packed in smoking a long time ago didn't help alleviate the odd tension. Neither did spotting Mikki.

She'd hung her overalls back on the peg and she was just standing there, her back towards Tama. She probably had no idea how the slump of her shoulders was advertising her state of mind as clearly as her expressions did.

Tama's need for a bit of solitude went head to head with the knowledge that he could—and should—do something to debrief their new recruit. She hadn't seen him, however. He could slip out the back door and find a quiet spot in the sun for a minute or two.

There would be plenty of time later for some reassurance and encouragement, but Tama had hesitated and then he was lost. With a sigh, he gave in to the pull that led him away from the back door.

'What *do* you think you're doing?'

Mikki jumped.

Oh, God! What had she done wrong *now*?

This day had started with such promise and excitement and now it was going from bad to worse, but she wasn't about to let Tama know how crushed she was feeling. She really didn't want to give him the satisfaction of having his doubts affirmed.

No. She knew that when the going got tough, that was when the tough had to get going. Mikki straightened her shoulders and lifted her chin before she turned to face Tama. She held his gaze and waited for whatever reprimand was coming. Ready to fight back, if necessary.

Her resolve to hold that eye contact wavered with the horrible thought that Tama could see way too much. There was something about those dark eyes that made her feel curiously defenceless. Whatever he saw, however, didn't seem to displease him because his mouth pulled to one side in a half-smile that was distinctly disconcerting. People didn't usually smile at you when they were about to tear you to shreds.

'We tend to leave our overalls on for the rest of the shift after the first callout,' he said. 'You never know what's coming next.'

'We'. He'd said 'we' as though he considered her to be one of the crew. Mikki took a careful inward breath and dampened the flash of hope that tiny word had created. Was he patronising her in some way? Did he really expect her to believe he didn't consider her an incompetent encumbrance after this morning's efforts?

Employing the benefit of the doubt would have been the wise thing to do but insecurity was deeprooted. She did do her best to sound offhand, to try and pretend it didn't matter. 'I thought you might prefer to leave me behind next time.'

'Why?'

'Well…' He *knew*, dammit. She could see it in his

eyes. Did he expect her to describe her inability to perform a lifesaving procedure? Spell it out in excruciating detail? Mikki could feel heat creeping up from her neck and heading towards her cheeks. 'I didn't exactly—'

'You did great,' Tama interrupted, sounding as casual as Mikki had been striving for. As though it was no big deal. 'It was a pretty full-on scene for your first callout.'

He was smiling with both sides of his mouth now and it connected to his eyes in a way that made them… warmer. It gave the impression he was being genuine but kindness seemed too much to expect. Inappropriate, somehow. Mikki could feel herself frowning as she tried to remember what had seemed so important a moment ago.

'I'd like to have done a better job with that intubation.'

The big man actually shrugged. 'We got there in the end.'

'*You* got there.'

'I got lucky.' Unexpectedly, Tama's eyes danced for a heartbeat. 'Plus, I knew it was a pig of a job. I went down two sizes in the ET tube.'

Mikki shut her eyes for a moment, both as a distraction from that disconcerting twinkle and to berate herself. Why hadn't she thought of that for her second attempt? With all the swelling and bleeding going on, it made perfect sense to downsize from what a patient of that build would normally need.

'Nice job with that IV,' Tama added. 'We could have lost that guy if we hadn't got fluids started soon enough. Tip someone into irreversible shock and it doesn't matter what fancy techniques you throw in later. They're still going to go into multi-organ failure and die.'

Mikki couldn't help staring. He *was* being nice to her. But why? If she had done outstandingly well the first time they had worked together in the field she might have understood. He hadn't been thrilled to have her on the team but if she had proved herself a valuable addition then at least acceptance, if not respect, might have been reasonable, but she hadn't done outstandingly well. Anyone could put in an IV.

Tama was still talking about it. 'Bit different for you, to say the least. You don't have someone trapped in awkward positions in ED and a dozen impatient firemen breathing down your neck.'

Her mind was racing at a million miles an hour. Tama was being kind. Glossing over something he could have used to her disadvantage, even to the point of refusing to take her on missions for the foreseeable future. Instead, he was glossing over the failure and focussing on what she had achieved. It came across a bit like someone patting a child on the head and telling them they'd done well just because you could see they'd done their best.

Was it because he was responsible for training her and that schedule had a certain number of boxes to get ticked? And the sooner they were done, the sooner Tama's involvement would be over? Maybe he didn't care about the quality of his trainee's work as much as getting his sentence as a mentor done and dusted.

Still…Mikki dredged up a smile and turned to unhook her overalls from the peg. This was the second chance she wanted, wasn't it? She couldn't afford to be oversensitive about the motives for which it was being offered.

'Get changed fast,' Tama advised finally. 'Lunch is getting cold.'

So that was that. The incident had been discussed and was to be forgotten. Mikki had been on her first callout and was that much closer to becoming an accepted crew member.

Her spirits lifted even further when her training continued after a short meal break. Mikki practised loading and unloading gear from the back of the helicopter. Hooking straps into place and checking they were secure. Easing the foot end of the stretcher into slots where it could be locked into place.

Tama was an excellent teacher. He demonstrated the task to show her what the expected skills were and then he repeated the action slowly, pausing to explain exactly what he was doing and why. Then he showed her again, at normal speed, with just a few key words to remind her of what needed to happen.

'Unclip here. Slide. Lift. Use your legs, not your back.'

Mikki did her best but had to growl in frustration when it came to the stretcher.

'My legs are too short. I can't reach properly.'

'Bend from the hips to give yourself a longer stretch. Bring one knee up and support yourself on the floor. The knees of the overalls are padded so it's safe to kneel even at an accident site.'

'Hey!' Mikki could reach and push far more easily. She flipped the locking mechanism over the stretcher handle. 'That worked.' She beamed.

Tama was watching with what appeared to be an equal measure of satisfaction. With her performance or his advice?

'Your legs reach the ground,' he said blandly. 'Just the right length if you ask me.'

It was just a moment in time. A couple of heartbeats, but it was long enough to feel *too* long. As though something was being said that had nothing at all to do with the task in hand.

Or was she being over-sensitive again? Reading more into the interaction with her mentor because there was something about him that was so dangerously attractive?

Mikki dragged an unwilling line of vision away. Seeking distraction. She found it way above Tama's head.

'What's that?'

'What?' Tama turned his head.

'That…platform thing with the ladder.' She pointed to the far corner of the hangar's roof.

'It's a simulator. For winch training. That's a skid and that pole thing that's folded in at the moment is a boom.'

'So you can hang from that? In a harness?'

'You have to do some groundwork first. Learn how to use the harnesses and work with carabiners and what hand signals mean and so on. *Then* we start using the simulator.'

Mikki's upward gaze was rapt. 'Cool!'

'Don't get too excited.' His tone was a warning. 'Not everybody gets to do winch training and it'll be a while before I'm ready to make a decision as to whether or not *you're* a suitable candidate. Months, probably.'

Mikki just nodded. She didn't want to catch Tama's gaze and read a reminder that she hadn't particularly impressed him with her skills so far. The silence that fell could have become awkward but the hangar door opened in the nick of time to admit the station manager, Andy.

'HUET tomorrow,' he informed Tama.

'What? That's not supposed to be on the agenda until next month.'

'They brought it forward. Did you not see last week's memo? The gear's needed somewhere else next month. There's no need to sound quite so unenthusiastic either. You knew it was coming.'

'Yeah…but not tomorrow! We're on duty.'

'Relief crew's coming in. They're doing their training the following day. No excuses,' Andy ordered. 'You know how important this is, Tama, and you know it doesn't happen very often. We go when we're told.' He smiled at Mikki. 'You get to do it, too,' he said. 'You're lucky. This only happens once every couple of years. We have to get the gear flown in from Australia for this and it's a big deal. Great opportunity for you.'

Mikki had no idea what he was talking about but the enthusiasm was contagious. She returned the smile. 'That's great!'

'Tell Tama that,' Andy ordered, heading back to his office.

'You have no idea what he's talking about, do you?' Tama asked drily.

'No.' Mikki caught her bottom lip between her teeth. 'Hewy?'

'H.U.E.T.,' Tama spelt out. 'Stands for Helicopter Underwater Escape Training.'

'Oh…'

'There's a morning of theory in the classroom and then we get to go out to that sports complex where you did the pre-requisite. There'll be a crane beside the diving pool and it has a cage that's designed to replicate the fuselage and seating of a helicopter.'

Mikki could actually feel the sinking sensation in her heart. 'And it goes in the pool?' As if it hadn't been a big enough ask, running up and down the steps beside that pool.

'Yep.'

'With people inside?'

'Yep.'

'Wearing clothes? And helmets? In harnesses and safety belts?'

'Oh, yeah.'

'And we have to escape and get to the surface so we don't drown.'

'More than once. We get to do it vertical a couple of times and then it goes in vertical and gets flipped on one side. And while it's not compulsory, if you really want to get the most out of the training…' Tama's gaze was a steady challenge '…you can get turned completely upside down with or without blackout goggles.'

Good grief! This sounded like a lot more than she had bargained for in her training. The fear that might come from dangling from a winch line paled in comparison. Her heart skipped a beat and picked up speed but showing Tama how nervous the prospect made her feel was not an option.

She grinned. 'Talk about being thrown in the deep end!'

Tama didn't return the smile. 'This is serious,' he told her. 'And dangerous. You won't be forced to participate.'

'Sounds like an opportunity I'd be stupid to miss.' Mikki lifted her chin. 'I'll give it a go. Do we take turns?'

'No. It's crew training. We'll all be in the crate together.'

Tama's expression was controlled to the point of appearing empty but Mikki had no trouble interpreting what was going on behind those dark eyes. A female crew member who panicked and made the training even more dangerous for anyone else would be more than a liability.

She would be history.

Mikki swallowed hard, aware of goose-bumps rising on her arms. She had wanted a second chance to prove herself to this man. This may be bigger and scarier than any situation she would have preferred and it might not showcase any medical skills but this was it.

And, dammit, she was going to show Tama James what she was made of.

They were almost done.

A bedraggled knot of people—Tama, Josh, Steve and Mikki—stood on the side of the diving pool. They were wearing float suits, which were like their overalls with the addition of a special lining, but enough water had seeped in over the last hour to chill them and they all shivered occasionally as they listened to the man in charge of this practical session of their HUET.

'You've done well,' he was saying. 'I'm impressed, guys. Especially with you, Mikki, given that you've only just started working with choppers.'

'Th-thanks.' The attempt to suppress a shiver failed but Mikki was smiling as she pushed back the sopping length of her braid that was still sending a trickle of water to drip off the pads of her life jacket.

Her dive mask was pushed to the top of her head and it made her face seem smaller. Her features were as delicate and perfectly proportioned as the rest of her body, Tama realised. He also had the thought that from any kind of a distance you would have considered this to be a child playing dressup. He was close enough to see the mature and steely determination in those blue eyes, however, and so far she had lived up to whatever standard she had deemed necessary.

Mikki had exceeded his expectations, that was for sure.

She'd sat quietly, strapped into the seat, as they'd been lowered into the pool for the first time. She had remembered to hold her breath until the bubbles had cleared and that had been the only occasion she had fumbled at all with releasing her harness. She'd stayed admirably calm on the next try, managing to open the door herself when she had a turn on that side of the 'fuselage'.

Even having the crate rotated on their last attempt hadn't fazed her, but the real test was coming. Now, when they were cold and feeling the kind of exhaustion that came after bodies were pushed to keep releasing high levels of adrenaline. The instructor was thinking ahead as well.

'This one's the biggie,' he warned. 'Upside down. You've got to hold your breath, release your harness, find the door and orient yourself before you swim to the surface.' He was looking at Mikki. 'This isn't compulsory, any more than the blackout goggles are. It's your call.'

Would she do it? Tama wouldn't blame her if she declined. She'd proved herself already as far as he was concerned. Outstandingly quick in the classroom and gutsy as hell so far in the practical.

'Mikki?' The instructor had moved so that he towered over the shortest member of the crew. 'You've probably done enough for your first HUET. Want to call it quits for the day and get warm and dry?'

Mikki didn't hesitate. 'No,' she said.

Tama exchanged a meaningful glance with Josh and mirrored the raised eyebrows but hid his grin.

Go, the mouse!

'I want to do it,' Mikki added firmly. 'I'd rather find out how tough it is in a controlled environment than in some lake or out at sea.'

It was ridiculous to feel so proud of her. Puzzling, in fact. Tama knew he was frowning as he spoke up.

'I don't want Mikki by the door. We need someone who's confident of opening it fast.'

'You want that spot?'

'Sure. I'll have some goggles, too, thanks.'

'Right. Let's get into this, guys. I reckon you'll all be pretty keen to get this over and done with.'

He wasn't wrong.

Tama had done this before but he still felt a flutter of nerves with the lurch as the crate was swung up and then over the deep pool. Maybe those nerves were there *because* he had done it before. From knowing how easily panic could claw at you and how hard it could be to fight it taking hold. How incredibly disorienting it was to be upside down underwater.

His senses were heightened by wearing the blackout goggles. He could hear the shouts of people poolside, operating the machinery or just watching in fascination. He could smell the chlorine and feel the chafe of wet clothing and the heaviness of his boots.

And he could sense Mikki strapped into the seat beside his position near the door. Steve and Josh were in the front seats of this skeletal 'helicopter'. It was just Tama and Mikki here at the back and he was even more aware of how tiny she was. Fragile? Not on your life. Vulnerable? Quite possibly. Wasn't everybody in some circumstances?

Slowly, the crate was turned until they were upside down. Hanging in their harnesses with blood rushing to their heads and effort needed to stop limbs dangling inconveniently. For a moment, Tama regretted opting for the blackout goggles. With the next lurch that signified their descent came a real flash of concern for Mikki. He wanted to be able to see her to gauge how she was coping with hanging like this. Whether she had any idea at all that this was about to get one hell of a lot harder.

Right...*now*...as their heads reached water level and the downward momentum continued.

Tama remembered to keep his mouth shut and hold his breath. He may not be able to see the bubbles escaping but he could hear them and feel them. It was like being immersed in a huge effervescent drink. He waited until it was quiet and still. And in that moment of quiet, with everything totally black came something like a faint wash of panic. Not for himself. For the princess.

Because, despite the short length of their acquaintanceship, Tama knew perfectly well that Mikayla Elliot did not have a princess mentality, no matter what her background was. She was tiny but, man, she was tough. Currently a lone female in a male world. An ultimately feminine one at that. Her size gave her the pathos of the runt of the litter. Her career choice made her a maverick.

They had that in common, didn't they? Never mind that her sheer guts had earned his genuine respect. He had the feeling there were more surprises in store with this woman and he didn't want to miss out on any of them. Most of all, right now he didn't want anything bad to happen to her.

With more haste than he would otherwise have employed, Tama used one hand to unclip his harness and with the other hand he reached for the door control and unlocked it. He shoved the door open. Now he should pull himself through it, turn the right way up and kick for the surface before his lungs started to really complain about the lack of fresh oxygen.

He couldn't do it. With no vision, he couldn't be sure that Mikki had freed herself from her harness. She'd had that momentary fumble on the first try, hadn't she? The rocking of the crate and sounds he could hear all seemed to be generated from the space Steve and Josh were occupying.

Those sounds diminished rapidly. Within seconds, Tama instinctively knew it was just himself and Mikki left in this crate, under metres of water. He could imagine Josh and Steve breaking the surface and climbing from the pool. Joining the spectators to watch and wait for the remaining crew members. How long before they started to feel anxious? For alarm to become apparent? For someone to jump in and rescue Mikki?

Keeping one hand on the doorframe to keep himself oriented, Tama pushed back and then extended his other arm.

Feeling for Mikki. Ready to unclip her harness and haul her to safety if necessary.

It didn't matter a damn if she needed assistance to complete this assignment. It's what he would do for any crew member if this was for real, wasn't it?

And, dammit, Mikki was part of *his* crew now.

* * *

The hand touched her just as panic threatened to turn Mikki's brain to mush and make her cry out for help, even with the background knowledge that the action would speed up the process of drowning.

She reached out with her hand and found it grasped securely. With her other hand she finally managed to unclip her harness and wriggle free.

Tama was pulling her forward.

To safety.

Her lungs hurt. She couldn't tell which way was up and if Tama hadn't had hold of her hand she could have been in real trouble. His upward kick as she cleared the crate was strong enough to propel them both towards the surface but it took a fraction too long. Mikki's lungs gave up the struggle to hold her breath a fraction too early. She took some water in with that first frantic gulp of air and began coughing and spluttering.

'You OK, Mouse?'

Tama had his arms right around her and it took a moment for Mikki to realise she was clinging to his neck as he trod water out in the middle of the dive pool. She tried to answer but couldn't speak yet. She tried to move but Tama's hold tightened.

'Be still,' he advised calmly. 'Get your breath back.'

There was something so gentle in that command to 'be still' that Mikki found herself transfixed. Almost hypnotised.

Their heads were so close.

Close enough to kiss.

Where had *that* come from? Involuntarily, Mikki's gaze dropped to Tama's mouth and desire hit somewhere deep in her belly with the kick of a mule. He had the most *kissable* mouth she'd ever seen. Lips that looked so soft but had such firm lines. Lines that were currently crooked with one side pulled up into a hint of a smile.

Mikki's gaze shot up to find Tama watching her very steadily. His gaze dropped to *her* mouth.

Oh…Lord! Had he guessed what she'd been thinking about? And the way he was looking back at her now… was it possible he'd been thinking the same thing?

Yes.

If they'd been alone, Mikki would swear he would have kissed her at that moment. And she would have wanted him to. But they were far from alone and remembering that finally made Mikki aware of the sounds around them. The spectators' noise level was increasing. They were clapping.

Cheering, even.

The realisation of what she had just achieved hit home. She had confronted real danger and won. That flood of adrenaline and pure excitement came from winning the challenge, didn't it? Cheating death.

The sheer thrill of being alive. Of feeling so alive that every cell in your body seemed to be humming. It had nothing to do with the feel of Tama's arms around her body or that tiny fantasy she'd just experienced about kissing him.

OK, maybe it had a little bit to do with that. Physical attraction was another way of making your body feel alive, but it was just the icing on the cake that had led Mikki on this career path. The pursuit of this thrill.

Mikki was still holding Tama's gaze and…and it was like looking into a mirror.

He understood.

Here was someone else who recognised that thrill. Not reckless enough to chase it for its own sake but who could appreciate its benefits. Knew it was the most excitement life had to offer. Maybe he also shared the knowledge that, while physical attraction and fulfilment could be an added thrill, it could never be allowed to get in the way of experiencing the best.

Tama's eyes widened and there was a flash of something more than surprise as he clearly recognised the reflection. He let her go so they could both swim to the side of the pool but the knowledge of a real connection was still there and Mikki knew it wasn't something that was going to be broken easily.

CHAPTER FIVE

THE face behind the Perspex window of the helicopter got smaller.

It was too high now to be sure of where he was looking, but the downward tilt of Tama's head suggested that he was still watching Mikki, well after the hand he'd raised to return her wave had been lowered.

The way she was still watching him as the wash from the rotors faded and she was able to push back the wayward curls that had been teased from their restraint.

The way they had both been watching each other for the last two days. Stealing extra glances whenever there was a chance of them being undetected.

Awareness, that's what it was.

They were on new ground now. A foundation of mutual respect. Not that Mikki had had an opportunity to prove much in the way of her clinical skills because every job in the last two days had been a potential winch situation and she'd been left behind on station.

There'd been plenty of downtime as well, however, and Mikki had used it well. Just before this mission had been dropped on the crew, she had been demonstrating the hand signals she'd learned while they'd lounged in the armchairs of the messroom. She stood between the men and the huge television where a replay of a recent rugby game was on.

'Wind direction,' she announced, holding both arms extended to one side. 'I face the helicopter and point my arms towards the landing zone with the wind at my back.'

'Excellent,' Josh told her. Mikki acknowledged the praise with a quick smile as she moved into a new position.

'Move forward,' she said, using both arms in front and together with a pulling motion. 'Or move back.' With palms at right angles to her wrists, she pushed the air in front of her.

It was while she was demonstrating the 'do not land' signal of each arm straight out horizontally and then swung overhead that Mikki shifted her gaze from the approving smile still on Josh's face to notice that Tama's gaze was not following the movement of her hands.

He was staring at her *chest*!

It should have made Mikki angry. It would have if she'd been demonstrating something to anyone else and had noticed a completely inappropriate focus that could be deemed sexist. Demeaning, in fact.

What was disturbing about this was that her reaction was nothing like anger. It felt like having fuel poured over a spark she seemed incapable of extinguishing. A tickle of desire that was so pleasurable it was addictive.

And growing.

This new foundation was not simply a matter of the respect she'd earned during the HUET. It was coloured by the connection they'd discovered.

An awareness that was only a hair's breadth from being an irresistible attraction. Made all the more irresistible by the thought that someone like Tama could find someone like *her* interesting. Heady stuff. A drug that was tempting Mikki to go back to it again and again. To test its effect. To see if she would become resistant.

She would have expected Tama to have dismissed it by now but, instead, it seemed to be growing. Feeding on itself. An appetite that could become an addiction because it was apparently being fed from both sides by stolen glances and an appreciation of the information they were gathering.

'Shut down,' Mikki ordered briskly, making a 'cut-throat' gesture with her right hand.

Tama's gaze flew up and Mikki could see that she had startled him out of whatever direction his thoughts had been travelling. She could also see the faint query in his eyes and then a twinkle that blatantly said he knew he'd been busted and didn't care.

Damn it! That sheer confidence in combination with that mischievous twinkle was just adding power to a magnetic pull. One that Mikki simply had to resist. This man was her mentor, for heaven's sake. She was here to gather the skills she needed for the next step in a carefully planned career. A fling—however thrilling it might be—was not an option. It would either distract her from what she needed to learn or it would end in tears and possibly ruin the only chance she was going to get to have this training. Definitely ruin the opportunity she had of learning from the best in the field.

But did she even have grounds to worry? Tama James had to be the most career-focussed man she'd ever met. More passionately involved with his work than many registrars she'd worked with who were consumed by ambition to make a consultant's position in the shortest possible time.

No way would he risk his job, and doing something as inappropriate as having a sexual relationship with his pupil would definitely land him in very hot water.

'Clear to start engine.' Mikki raised her right arm and drew circles in the air above her head. She extended her arms sideways. 'Clear to lift.' Then she raised them high with her thumbs clear of her fists. 'Take off,' she instructed.

And, right on cue, the pagers sounded and both men jumped up from their chairs.

Josh gave Mikki a suspicious glance. 'That was spooky. You got a hot line to Control or something?'

'Feminine intuition,' she responded. 'One of the benefits of having a chick on the crew.'

'One of many, I'm sure,' Tama murmured as he walked past, but Mikki didn't dare meet his gaze.

Going any further down that conversational path would be blatant flirting. Playing the dangerous game of exploring the edges of an existing attraction was one thing. Encouraging it would be insane. The rules of this game were quite clear. If awareness and attraction were building blocks, they could do what children who weren't friends could do. Check out the shapes and colours of the blocks. Shift them around a little and make pleasing shapes. Parallel play.

What they could *not* do was play together. To make anything that would undoubtedly lead to joining more than building blocks.

'I hope this isn't going to be another winch job,' she

said casually as she followed the men into the office where they would get details of the mission and do the initial map work.

But it was and again Mikki was left on station to keep herself busy. Not that there was any shortage of options. The stack of articles Tama had copied for her sat on a coffee-table near where he'd been sitting, and Mikki picked up one of the few she hadn't read yet titled 'Air Medical Transport of the Cardiovascular Patient'.

She sat down with every intention of absorbing what she needed to know concerning aspects such as the risk of patient deterioration due to a decrease in barometric pressure with rising altitude.

Was it her imagination that the soft cushions of this chair were still warm from their previous occupant? That there was a faint, musky, very masculine scent surrounding her?

Whatever. It was enough to make Mikki pull her feet up and curl deeper into the chair, oblivious to the faint smile curving her lips.

'Cardiac reserve,' she muttered aloud, her tone resigned. 'The ability of the heart to increase output in response to increased demands.'

For the first time, as he watched the figure on the ground get smaller and smaller, Tama felt a pang of disappointment that Mikki had been left behind.

Had it really only been last week when he'd been wishing so fervently for a mission that would enable escape from her company?

Josh seemed to be reading his mind as Steve banked the helicopter and their forward speed increased.

'Damn shame the mouse couldn't come.'

'It's an injured tramper. We're not likely to find a close landing space in that kind of bush.'

'Get her winch trained, then,' Steve suggested. 'I'll bet she's keen.'

'It's way too early to even think about that,' Tama growled.

His colleagues were silent for a moment. Wondering why he was in a bad mood perhaps? And who was he trying to convince, anyway? Them or himself?

'She's capable enough,' Josh said. 'Look at the way she threw herself into the HUET. Amazing!'

Tama simply grunted. They could think what they liked about his mood. He wasn't about to admit his total agreement. Not out loud, that's for sure. No reason not to let his mind play along those lines, though.

The princess was amazing all right and not just for the physical courage she had displayed during the underwater escape training.

She hadn't whinged once about being left behind on mission after mission. She'd been using her time constructively to devour the pile of written material Tama had actually intended to daunt her. All those heavy articles on the conditions they could be expected to transport and considerations that came with treating complications at high altitude and in a confined space.

Josh broke into his thoughts. 'You know, it could be useful to have a doc who's winch trained.'

'Why?'

'There's stuff she'd be qualified to do that we can't.'

The disturbing notion that Dr Elliot could end up being better at this job than he was hadn't occurred to Tama.

'Like what?' he snapped.

'Oh, I dunno. Amputations?'

'We can take on-line direction for treatment that's out of our protocols if it's a last resort.'

'Yeah, but how much time does it take to find a doctor who can talk us through something like that? And what about, say, a thoracotomy?'

'Cracking a chest in the field? Are you kidding? Just how likely do you think it would be for someone to survive that?'

'They do it in ED.'

'Almost never. And they generally have a cardiothoracic surgeon to do the procedure and a theatre to tidy up in afterwards.' Tama knew he was being dismissive. Probably sounding more and more grumpy, but he didn't like the idea of Mikki ending up better than him. To have something he'd worked for so damn hard handed to her on a plate—like everything else in her life.

'Hey, I'm just saying.' Josh shook his head, abandoning the conversation. 'I reckon the mouse would be good to have around, that's all. She's really into the whole helicopter scene.' He grinned at Tama. 'She's got the hand signals down pat, you have to admit that.'

'Yeah.'

Tama turned his head to stare down at the ground. They were approaching the rugged, bush-covered hills that lay between the city and the coastline. Somewhere down there lay an injured tramper who was probably hypothermic by now because it had taken his friend a good few hours to walk out and call for help.

That's what he should be thinking about. Not replaying the mental footage of Mikki standing in front of them, her face a mixture of satisfaction and an eagerness to impress, moving her body like some football team's head cheerleader.

It wasn't just the hand signals she'd mastered, though, was it?

She'd also learned the layout of the back of the helicopter by now and could find anything in the Thomas pack in no time flat. It had been fun testing her yesterday.

'Find a large trauma dressing.

'Where are the spare batteries?'

It could have been a game judging by the smile with which Mikki produced whatever she was asked to find.

'Magill forceps.

'Chest decompression kit.

'Sharps container.'

She got fast enough to need more of a challenge.

'A tourniquet, 16-gauge cannula, wipe, luer plug and tegaderm. Set up a running line of 0.9 per cent saline while I'm pretending to get the IV access.'

Not a peep came out of Mikki about why it might have been more appropriate for *her* to be the one putting a line in while Tama assisted by setting up fluids.

Unlike Josh, she'd never suggested it could be worthwhile accelerating her training because she could do more in the field than he was authorised to do.

In fact, not once since she'd set foot on their station had she pulled rank in any way. She hadn't used her superior qualifications, any limitations that would have been perfectly reasonable given her gender, or any status associated with who her father happened to be.

He'd been expecting her to, he realised now. Ready to fight back. He wouldn't have been at all surprised if the boss had called him in for a quiet word because Mikki had said something to her father and he wanted to make sure his daughter got everything she wanted.

Had she not said anything? How often did she talk to her father? Did she know that Tama knew who he was? His colleagues had agreed with him right from the start that Mikki was to be treated like any other trainee and it would be better not to even mention her family connections so maybe she didn't realise they knew.

Were they both keeping that knowledge as a kind of ace up their sleeves? Would Mikki use hers first? Tama had to admit he was impressed that she hadn't let anything slip. But, then, that admiration that had started so grudgingly had taken on a life of its own, hadn't it?

Hell, even if this woman had resembled a potato in her physical appearance, Tama would have been impressed by now.

And she didn't look anything like a potato.

She looked…amazing.

Tama sighed aloud. There it was, in a nutshell. He was attracted to her…big-time.

Josh had overheard the sigh. 'Getting bored, mate? We're almost there.'

'Never bored,' Tama's smile at his friend was a kind of apology for his distraction. 'Bring it on!'

OK. He was attracted to Mikki, but did it matter? He wasn't going to act on it. The very idea was ludicrous. She was here to learn. From him. That put him in the position of being her superior. Her teacher. Ethically, he would be on dodgy ground if he let any kind of relationship interfere with that.

And he didn't do relationships. Especially not with

someone like Mikki. She was so not his type it was almost funny. Relationships meant you got close to someone, and if Mikki knew his background she'd look down on him. She wouldn't be able to help herself. Just part of her social programming.

No. Tama liked where he was. He liked the respect—admiration, even—he could read in Mikki's face. His past was his own so it was good that there was a very large barrier that would prevent him acting on his attraction. He didn't need to think of getting that close.

Hey…nobody got that close so why the hell was he even thinking about it?

Because Mikki had got under his skin, that's why. Far enough to make him miss her when she wasn't around. There was no harm in appreciating the woman, though, was there? Playing a little?

Admitting the attraction was a release in a way. He knew what he was up against and he could handle it. From here on in, it was not going to distract him from the important things, like doing his job. This job, for instance. They were circling the area the GPS navigation system had identified. Any minute now and they would be into the rescue effort. Everything was good.

And if the next job meant that they had the mouse along to play, so be it. Tama could handle that, too.

The strident sound of the pagers came within minutes of the helicopter touching down but Tama appeared to be taking the details of the call with good humour.

Mikki was watching him.

She'd watched the helicopter land and Tama and Josh climb out, laughing and talking as they'd made their way back inside. It had been so good to see them. Because she'd spent two hours studying and had had enough?

Yes, but that didn't explain the way her heart tripped when she saw the now familiar shape of Tama heading her way. Her excitement wasn't just about having stimulating company on station or the prospect of a new job that would include her in the action.

She had missed Tama's presence. Missed the way he filled a room and gave even the air she breathed an extra dimension. He was larger than life, that was the problem. More so than any man she'd ever met. Some of that aura radiated and it was almost like the kind of adrenaline rush you got from facing a major challenge and succeeding.

It made her feel…bigger, somehow. Taller and braver and…special.

Tama wasn't looking at her right now as he talked to the dispatcher and scribbled down the co-ordinates he was being given. His head was bent and Mikki indulged herself for a second longer, her eyes feasting on the way tiny curls spiralled against the soft-looking skin at the nape of his neck. A vulnerable spot on a man who seemed anything but vulnerable. It made Mikki want to touch it. To touch *him*. She dragged her gaze away as Tama turned to hand the scrap of paper with numbers on it to Josh, who moved towards the wall maps.

'Roger,' he said finally. 'We'll get airborne as soon as we've refuelled.'

'Another job?' The question was redundant. Stupid, in fact, but Mikki couldn't help asking it. Knowing that Tama would look in her direction when he answered. Wanting him to notice her.

The smile was a bonus she hadn't expected. 'Tractor rollover,' he told her. 'Forty-two-year-old farmer.'

'Is he trapped?'

'No, and the ground was reasonably soft by the sound of things, but he's got chest injuries and the local ambulance crew is concerned about his breathing.'

'How far?'

Josh was using his finger to trace lines on one of the large wall maps. 'Here. Fifteen- to twenty-minute flight, tops.'

'And it's not a winch job.' Tama actually sounded quite cheerful about the fact. 'You good to go, Mouse?'

'Absolutely.'

Finally. The frustration of the last few days evaporated and Mikki was left with a sense that the enforced time on station had actually been a blessing in disguise. She was familiar with the gear and the protocols. Far more at ease with these men. Confident, even.

It felt so right to be keeping step with Tama despite having to take much longer strides to stay by his side. Perfectly normal to climb into her seat, fasten her safety straps—lap belt first and then shoulder straps—and then glance up to be rewarded with an approving nod. This time, she actually felt like part of the team and that impression only strengthened when they arrived at the scene.

'This is John.' The local ambulance officer introduced them to their patient. 'He lost control of the tractor on that hill and it rolled. He was caught under it and then thrown clear when it rolled again.'

The tractor was lying on its side, half in a ditch, close to where the ambulance was parked.

'Steering…wheel…' John groaned. 'Got…me…'

'Don't try and talk, mate.' Tama had his hand on John's wrist, both to assess his pulse and convey reassurance through touch. 'We're going to look after you and get you to hospital, OK?'

John gave a single nod and then closed his eyes.

'I couldn't get a line in.' The ambulance officer sounded apologetic as he noticed Josh pulling supplies from the pack. 'His blood pressure was well down by the time I arrived. He's pretty flat.'

'You single-crewed?' Tama asked.

'Yes.' The ambulance officer was obviously relieved to have a crew with higher qualifications to take over. 'His airway was clear when I got here and there were no obvious signs of any neck injury. Breathing seemed OK, too. He said it hurt but his oxygen saturation was ninety-eight per cent.'

'Down to ninety-five now.' Josh dropped a tourniquet beside John's arm and handed a stethoscope to Mikki as though it was part of a practised team routine.

Mikki fitted the earpieces.

'What's his blood pressure now?' she queried.

'It's been a few minutes since I took it. It was eighty-five over sixty.'

'Narrow pulse pressure,' Tama commented. 'We're just going to have a look at your chest, John.'

The farmer didn't open his eyes. He seemed to be concentrating on drawing breath. Rapid, shallow breaths that looked laboured.

'Flail chest,' Mikki noted, as Tama pulled aside the woollen shirt and cut John's singlet with a pair of shears he pulled from a pouch on his overalls.

She watched for a moment longer, assessing the

section of rib cage that was being sucked in the opposite direction to the rest of his ribs. There were multiple fractures there and the list of potential damage that might accompany them was long.

'Have a listen,' Tama invited, moving to make room for Mikki to crouch closer to their patient. 'I'm going to check his belly.'

The injured part of the chest was on the left side. Low enough to make an internal injury to the spleen a distinct possibility, along with bleeding that could well be contributing to low blood pressure.

Josh was attempting to gain IV access and Tama's hands were palpating John's abdomen but Mikki focussed on what she was hearing with her stethoscope. Or not hearing.

'Breath sounds well down on the left side,' she reported. 'And heart sounds are muffled.'

'I can't find a vein,' Josh said. 'You want to try, Tama?'

'In a sec.' Tama was holding Mikki's gaze. 'What are you thinking?'

There was respect in that gaze. A willingness to let her make decisions about treating a man who was critically injured. Mikki didn't want control, however. She wanted teamwork.

'Narrow pulse pressure,' she said, instead of offering a diagnosis. 'Tachycardia. His jugular veins are distended, see?'

Tama glanced at the bulging veins in John's neck and nodded curtly. 'Tamponade?'

Mikki tapped the chest wall. 'Could be a tension pneumothorax. Or a combination of both.'

'Chest decompression or a pericardiocentesis?'

Mikki touched John's neck. 'No tracheal deviation.' Her gaze travelled to a face partially covered by an oxygen mask. 'He's going blue. What's the oxygen saturation now?'

'Ninety per cent.'

'John? Can you hear me?' Mikki rubbed his collarbone. 'Can you open your eyes?'

There was no response.

The farmer was in shock and deteriorating fast. If air was entering the chest outside the lungs because of trauma to the ribs, it could be compressing his heart and lung and would be fatal if that air wasn't removed. If he was bleeding around his heart as a result of the crush injury, that vital organ would cease to function and he would die very quickly.

'What would you do first?' she asked Tama.

'Your call,' he responded quietly. He wasn't testing her. She could see that he was weighing up exactly the same considerations she was. If one procedure didn't help, they would have to try another anyway. What was paramount was making a decision and getting on with it.

'Pericardiocentesis,' Mikki decided swiftly. 'Followed by a chest decompression if it's needed.'

'You happy to do it?'

Mikki nodded. 'I'd like a monitor on.'

There was a narrow space around the heart where blood could create enough pressure to stop it functioning. A space that was easy to miss with the point of a needle. Not going far enough would mean not removing the blood. Going too far would mean pushing a needle into cardiac tissue and potentially creating further complications.

Tama put the leads of the monitor on. Josh pulled out

the kit she needed. Mikki put on a fresh pair on gloves and didn't allow her thoughts to go anywhere near the idea of failure, even though this was technically a lot more difficult than an intubation.

'Keep an eye on the trace, please,' she asked Tama. 'I'm going in slowly and I want to know if you see any changes in rhythm.'

Their patient was unconscious. He didn't feel the needle entering his chest just under his breastbone. Mikki angled the needle at forty-five degrees, aiming for the left shoulder blade. She pulled back on the plunger as she kept advancing the needle.

'Ectopic,' Tama warned, his voice very close behind her. 'Ventricular.'

Mikki slowed. She was close. She pulled back on the plunger as she kept advancing the needle, a millimetre at a time.

'Bingo,' she said softly, seconds later. It was easy to draw back the plunger now. The syringe filled with blood. 'Twenty mils should be enough to make a difference if the tamponade's the main culprit.'

They all watched for a minute to see John's respiratory efforts improving and his blood pressure creeping up.

Another minute and he began to regain consciousness. Less than five minutes later they had intravenous access established, fluids running and their patient stable enough to transport. The short flight to the hospital was a busy time of reassessment, monitoring and further treatment and it wasn't until well after the handover to emergency department staff that Mikki discovered how impressed her colleagues were.

'He would've died if you hadn't been there,' Josh told her. 'That was awesome, Mikki Mouse.'

'It's an effective procedure when it's needed.' Mikki tried to sound modest. 'But it's not that different to a chest decompression for pneumothorax. I'm surprised you don't have it in your procedures.'

'It's coming in.' Tama's voice had a curiously rough edge as though the words were hard to get out. 'I wouldn't mind getting a head start on it, though.'

'I'll run through it with you on a manikin any time you like.'

'Cool.'

Josh wanted to discuss the case as they flew back to base. To go over the signs and symptoms and talk more about the lifesaving procedure, but Tama was curiously quiet. Mikki caught him watching her with an oddly assessing gaze.

Had she passed muster this time, perhaps?

She got the impression she had and the sheer joy that gave her was startling enough to make her want to sit quietly and savour it. She let Josh continue talking and just made the right noises when needed. Even after they landed and climbed out of the helicopter, Josh was still talking.

'Man, I'm starving,' he announced. 'Did we have lunch?' He didn't wait for Tama's response. 'So long ago it doesn't count, anyway. I'm going to make a mountain of toast.'

He set off towards the messroom.

Steve was still busy shutting down the helicopter.

Mikki was suddenly alone in the hangar with Tama and, without looking, she knew he was staring at her.

She ducked her head. 'I'm pretty hungry myself. I'll go and help Josh with that toast.'

'No.' The single word stopped her in her tracks. 'Wait a sec. I...want to talk to you.'

Mikki turned. That odd note was in his voice again. As though he was saying something he would rather not be saying but felt compelled to.

There was certainly something compelling about his gaze. Mikki couldn't look away.

Tama looked as though he was seeing her for the first time.

She could see respect.

Acceptance.

And something more.

Something that made her toes curl and her blood tingle.

It was Tama who broke the eye contact. Slowly. Deliberately. He cleared his throat and stared fixedly above her head. Mikki didn't follow his line of vision. She wanted to watch his face when he said whatever was important enough to make him look like this.

'I know you're keen,' he said gruffly. 'But I have to be seen to be careful about following the rules, you know?'

Keen? Mikki focussed on Tama's face, her mind one step ahead of him.

Dear Lord, he'd noticed the way she'd been watching him. The attraction wasn't mutual, as she'd thought, and he was about to tell her he couldn't teach someone who fancied him.

'But I've changed my mind,' Tama continued. 'If you really are that keen, we can...you know...do something about it. The boss doesn't need to find out.'

ALISON ROBERTS   87

The flush of colour entering Mikki's cheeks got
rapidly hotter. Was he offering her *sex*?

'How 'bout it?' Tama finally looked down and caught
her transfixed gaze.

'Ah…' Mikki couldn't think of a thing to say. Talk
about direct! 'Yes, please' might be equally direct and
honest, but it lacked a certain something.

Tama lowered his voice to a sexy rumble. 'You want
to, don't you?'

Oh…*help*! There was no denying that. And Tama
was doing that thing with his lips again. That quirky
half-smile that went with the twinkle Mikki was coming
to recognise. Pure mischief. She sucked in a breath.

'I guess I could…'

Her hesitation was all too plain.

'I know it's more than a bit out of order. Way too soon
and all that, but you know what?' The twinkle gained
intensity. 'I reckon you'll do OK.'

Mikki's jaw dropped. 'Oh…' Maybe she hadn't
measured up as well as she'd imagined.

Her reaction didn't seem to be what Tama had expected. He frowned. 'So…you want to start now?'

'*Now?*' Mikki squeaked. '*Here?*'

'Where else?' Tama was looking over her head
again. 'It's the only place I know of that's got a winch
simulator.'

CHAPTER SIX

'WINCH training? *Already?*'

'I'd barely started before we had our days off. I should be able to get into it properly this week. I'm lucky, Dad. Usually you have to wait *months* to get this sort of training.'

Mikki heard a deep sigh that travelled remarkably well, considering her father was currently on the other side of the world.

'I'm perfectly safe, Dad,' she said patiently. 'So far all I've been allowed to do is learn safety stuff and terminology and how to wear the harness and hook carabiners on and off things. My feet haven't left the ground and when they do, it'll only be in the hangar.'

'At the rate you're going, you'll be dangling out of a helicopter on a bit of string in no time.'

Mikki laughed. 'It's a wire capable of holding a ton of weight, as you well know. I'll bet you've done more research than I have about what's involved with helicopter crew training.'

Her father chuckled. 'Knowledge is power, you know.

I believe you've got bush and snow terrain survival training coming up as well. Do you know when?'

'No idea. I would imagine they wait for a group of trainees before that kind of operation. I'll have to ask Tama.'

'Tama,' her father repeated thoughtfully. 'Hmm…'

Mikki's mouth went suddenly dry. Could there be some kind of telepathic link being beamed by satellite? Surely there hadn't been any clue in her own tone or recent conversations to reveal how often that name echoed in her own head. Along with images that could stir up some rather disturbing physical effects. Good grief, what if her father knew that she had thought Tama was offering her sex instead of winch training?

That she might have been incapable of declining such an offer?

Or maybe there was another link. An equally disturbing one for some unidentifiable reason.

'You don't know him, do you, Dad?'

'No, of course not.' The response was lightning fast. 'Why would I?'

'You've been known to attend the odd fundraising function to do with helicopter rescue. Especially when you're handing over those big cheques. You just *sounded* like you'd heard the name before.'

'It's an unusual name, that's all.'

'He's part Maori.'

'And he's the senior crew member on your shift, yes?'

'Yes. And if I don't impress the pants off him, I won't get the qualification I want.'

'*What* did you say?'

Mikki groaned. 'Just an expression, Dad.'

'Hmm. Well, you're a big girl now. It's none of my business. What's he like, this Tama fellow, anyway?'

Unconsciously, Mikki licked her lips. This was like having a plate of comfort food put in front of you when you were cold and tired and hungry. An opportunity for her mind to feast on a whole smorgasbord of Tama's attributes.

Tall. Strong. Fierce. With the single-mindedness and determination of a warrior but with a thread of sensitivity that spoke of an equal ability to be gentle.

A streak of mischief that made dark eyes gleam and a smile that would melt the heart of any woman.

Someone who lived for challenge. For the thrill of revelling in how good it was to be alive and was prepared to do whatever it took to keep others alive.

A soulmate.

'He's the best,' she told her father simply. 'I couldn't have wished for a better teacher.'

Her father sighed again. 'You sound happy, anyway.'

'I *am* happy, Dad. I've never been happier. This is exactly what I've wanted to be doing for longer than I can remember.'

'Do you think there's any chance you'll get this danger-chasing business out of your system one of these days? Find a nice bloke and settle down, even? Preferably with someone who doesn't share your passion of leaping out of helicopters and saving lives?'

'I can pretty well guarantee that a nice bloke who's interested in a picket fence and a bunch of kids will not be leaping out of any helicopters.'

Someone like Tama 'settling down'? As if!

Her falling for someone who wanted the secure, ordinary life her father was thinking of?

Again, it was unlikely enough to be amusing.

'You're not even sixty, Dad. It's a bit young to be pining for grandchildren.'

The silence on the other end of the line made Mikki give herself a mental kick. Her father needed no reminder of how small his family was. Or how pining for someone had almost destroyed him in the years following her mother's death. Of the breeding ground for the over-protectiveness they still wrangled over.

Mikki caught a breath and made herself smile to ensure she sounded cheerful.

'I'll have to get to work soon, Dad. You haven't told me how it's going in New York. When do you have to get on a plane again? It's Zurich next, isn't it?'

The stack of materials was large and awkward to hold but Mikki's arms enclosed it willingly.

'You photocopied all this on your days off? And found all these videos and DVDs? Thank you *so* much!'

'No big deal.' Tama shrugged off the gratitude. He'd owed her one and he wasn't about to admit why. 'Some of it's as boring as hell, mind you. One of those videos is a lecture on the components and capabilities of winching gear. Way too many facts and figures to be interesting.'

'I'm interested,' Mikki assured him.

She was, too. Possibly in more than the kind of materials needed for her training. He'd been testing her the other day, hadn't he? Teasing her by not being specific about what he was offering. Playing with fire to find out whether she might be interested in *him*.

She'd been confused to start with, of course, but Tama had seen the signs of a response she probably hadn't known she'd been showing. The way her pupils had dilated, her breath quickening as her lips had parted slightly.

So damn hot, he'd had to step back before he could get burned. To stop the game before it had ended in tears. And then he knew he kind of owed her an apology and he wasn't quite sure how to offer it. He'd spent quite a lot of time on his days off thinking about it and by last night he'd come up with a perfect penance. He'd get all the resources she needed to make her training state of the art and he'd be there, every step of the way, to ensure her success.

'There's some good stuff in there as well. Practical demos on one of the DVDs. They've even filmed some real cases.'

'Fantastic. If you show me how to use the DVD player, I'll get into it the first time I get left on station.'

'What makes you think you'll be left behind?'

'If last shift was anything to go by, I'll have more than enough time to absorb this lot.'

'You're tempting fate, you know.'

'Ha!' Mikki shook her head, carrying her bundle of articles and audiovisual recordings towards the mess-room. 'You'll see.'

But it was Mikki who was proved wrong.

There were four missions that day and not one of them required the use of a winch.

They transferred a critically ill teenage girl from a rural hospital to an intensive care unit in the city, and Tama was struck by the rapport Mikki gained instantly with their patient. He watched the way she held the girl's hand during the flight and how their eye contact seemed to reassure and calm a terrified teenager.

The second job was time-consuming because they had to wait when it took longer than expected for a ski-rescue team to bring in a man who had collided with a tree and received head injuries. The injury had made their patient combative and Mikki was the target for some fairly colourful verbal abuse.

'Get her away from me. I don't want some female ambulance driver looking after me.'

'She's a doctor,' Tama told the man. 'She's more highly qualified than any of us.'

'I don't care. She's a woman. You can't trust any of them.'

Tama had seen resignation in Mikki's gaze as she'd stepped back. Concern for the man but acknowledgement that being assertive could distress him further and worsen his condition.

And he'd seen something else. Tama couldn't be sure what he'd read exactly in Mikki's eyes and face but he knew, beyond a shadow of a doubt, that their patient's impression was absolutely wrong.

Mikki could be trusted with anything. She was one hundred per cent genuine.

They went to an isolated farm where a three-week-old baby had contracted an infection and was in respiratory distress, and this time Tama could really appreciate Mikki's skills. Tama watched the confident, deft movements of hands that were half the size of his own as they located and managed to cannulate a tiny vein that looked like a thread.

Josh was watching just as closely and was clearly equally impressed with the feat, but Tama hoped his mind wasn't stepping in the same direction as his own. Just for a moment or two he couldn't help imagining how soft and sure the touch of those fingers would be. How it might be to experience that touch on his own skin.

Just the kind of distracting thought that would have annoyed the hell out of him a couple of weeks ago, but he could handle it now. Could enjoy the sensation and then put it aside—ready to help set up the monitoring equipment this baby badly needed.

Maybe he was getting used to dealing with a misplaced libido. Or maybe it was a combination of the confidence he had that he could deal with it added to the respect he was gaining for his pupil.

That respect went up a notch on the final job of the day. A car had gone off a coastal road and it could easily have been a winching job but the tide was out and beside the rocks was a stretch of firm sand that made an ideal place to land. The car was upside down and the single occupant was sprawled, face down, half on the back seat and half on the roof that was now the vehicle's floor. Totally out of reach.

'We'll have to wait for the fire service to cut access,' Tama decreed, but Mikki wasn't having any of it.

'I could fit through the window.'

'No way! Too dangerous.'

'Not if we knock the rest of the glass out. The car's stable enough, isn't it?'

'I guess.' The crumpled wreck was perfectly stable, wedged between two giant boulders. Tama was curiously reluctant to allow Mikki to squeeze into the tiny gap of a windowframe, however.

'Ignition's off. Fire danger should be low and it's an old car. There won't be any undeployed airbags. Not in the back, anyway.'

Tama turned to the chief fire officer, who was now standing beside him. 'It'll take us a few minutes to set up for cutting.'

'At least let me get in to make sure his airway's open,' Mikki pleaded.

The fire officer grinned. 'Keen, isn't she?'

'Yeah.' And suddenly Tama was proud of how brave Mikki was. Could appreciate her diminutive size. 'OK, go for it, Mouse. We'll pass in whatever you need.'

By the time they freed the victim, he was set to go, with a neck collar in place, oxygen on and IV fluids running.

She was good.

So good it no longer seemed premature to take her a step further in her training. Winch work, for sure, as soon as they could fit it in. Tama was going to sit down and have a good look at his calendar tonight as well. A clear day or two and he would start the preparations needed to give Mikki her survival training.

Why did frustration seem to be an inherent part of this job?

Was it just that Mikki wanted too much, too soon?

Last shift she'd been frustrated because she'd been left behind on station and had had to use her time to study. This shift the opposite was happening. Three busy days so far and she'd gone on every mission because not one of them had needed winching.

And it was frustrating because she wanted to soak in

all the background information Tama had provided for her on winching. She'd had her evenings, of course, but it wasn't the same as being able to fire questions at Tama as they occurred to her. Something as practical as playing with the simulator was as far away as it had ever been.

Mikki knew perfectly well that hindsight would make her appreciate this full-on spell. Already, she could see that both Tama and Josh had come to trust her judgement and recognise her strengths. They simply handed her the IV gear now and her opinion on every case was always sought. They had gelled together as a team even before the milestone of their tenth mission together that had been clocked up late yesterday.

But today was the last of their four-day shift and Mikki didn't want a stretch of days off when she was no closer to her new goal of being winch capable, so she was striding into the hanger with a purposeful step, a little earlier than usual, intent on persuading Tama to start her practical training.

The hangar was dimly lit with the new day just gathering strength, but the light was not dim enough to hide the two figures who were standing near the helicopter.

Both Tama and the station manager, Andy, were watching her with a focus that was unsettling, to say the least.

'Something wrong?' Mikki queried, by way of a greeting.

'Yeah.' Tama's scowl deepened. 'Josh won't be in to work today.'

'He's sick?'

'Not exactly.'

'He was out running last night,' Andy told her. 'This

MILLS & BOON
Pure reading pleasure

My Account / Offer of the Month / Our Authors / Book Club / Contact us

All of the latest books are there PLUS

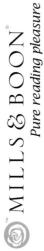

- Free Online reads
- Exclusive offers and competitions
- At least 15% discount on our huge back list
- Sign up to our free monthly eNewsletter

- More info on your favourite authors
- Browse the Book to try before you buy
- eBooks available for most titles
- Join the M&B community and discuss your favourite books with other readers

Take a look at what's on offer at
www.millsandboon.co.uk

idiot took a corner too fast, went off the road, through a fence and into the park Josh was running in.'

'Oh, my God,' Mikki breathed. 'He got *hit*?'

'Leg broken in three places,' Tama said gloomily. 'Femur, tib and fib, and his foot got squashed. He was in surgery for three hours.'

'He'll be in hospital for weeks,' Andy added. 'Off work for months.'

Mikki stood still, absorbing the bad news. Josh was a part of her team now. A friend. He'd been Tama's partner for a long time, too, and part of her concern and sympathy had to go to her mentor who would, no doubt, have to work with someone he didn't know nearly as well for quite some time.

Tama seemed to read and accept her mixed response. 'At least it wasn't his head,' he said quietly. 'He'll come right.'

Mikki nodded. 'Is he allowed visitors yet?'

'We'll go and annoy him every time we're at the hospital.'

'But…' A new concern emerged. 'What's going to happen today? With the crew, I mean?' Would a stranger be ready to accept her as a third crew member? Make her an integral part of the team the way Tama and Josh had?

'I was going to call in a replacement,' Andy said. 'But it was looking like we might have to stand you guys down. Then I thought of my old mate, Alistair.'

'Ex-helicopter crew,' Tama put in. 'Before my time.'

'Yes. He's retired from helicopter work,' Andy continued, 'but his qualifications are still current. He's got a website design business now that's quite portable. He's happy to hang out on station and be available for any winch jobs. Only operating the winch, mind you.' Andy chuckled. 'He says he's over dangling. He can still do his normal work on station. It's a fairly unusual arrangement but I've managed to clear it.'

'For any jobs that don't require winching,' Tama finished, 'I've told Andy that I'm more than happy to crew with you.'

Andy was frowning. 'It's kind of a big ask this soon in your training, Mikki. I said we'd have to see how you felt about it.'

'I…I'm happy if Tama's happy,' Mikki said slowly. She caught Tama's gaze, knowing that her questions would be written on her face.

You really want this? You trust me to be your partner?

The dark eyes were steady on hers. Warm.

Yes, they said. *You can do this. We can do this.*

'I'm happy,' was all Tama said.

Andy gave a nod. 'Let's see how it goes, then.' He smiled at Mikki. 'Tama tells me he wants to accelerate your training to include winching, but don't go getting any ideas that you'll be allowed to do anything in the near future.' He was looking at Tama. 'Safety first, remember?'

Tama cleared his throat. 'How could I forget?' he muttered. Then he smiled at Mikki. 'No time like the present, is there? Good thing you got to work early, Mouse.'

It was and it wasn't.

One frustration faded only to be replaced by a new one.

An unexpectedly fierce and potentially problematic one.

It started with Tama's first words when Andy had gone back to his office.

'Let's get a nappy on you, then,' he said.

'The harness, I hope.' Mikki hoped the light response would hide something more than embarrassment at the terminology. The very idea of Tama touching her in places that a nappy would cover was more than enough to send a flood of colour to her cheeks.

'We use a nappy harness by preference.' Tama was sorting through a box of gear in the corner of the hangar. 'Much more dangerous winching someone in a stretcher. Get a good spin or something going and it can be hard to control. Here.' He was holding out a collection of straps and fasteners. 'We'll pretend you're the patient. I'll just put my harness on first.'

The moment his hands touched Mikki's waist to put her harness in place she knew she was in trouble. She actually had to close her eyes as he reached for the wide strap that went between her legs and his hands brushed the insides of her thighs.

'Don't mind me.' She could hear the grin in his voice.

She tried to smile back. To appear as nonchalant as Tama sounded, but her heart was hammering and her lips felt frozen.

She knew this sensation. Kind of. She'd only ever experienced a pale imitation of this, however. Lust, pure and simple.

She *didn't* mind. Far, far from it.

She wanted more.

Heaven help her, but she wanted that touch on her thighs without the barrier of clothing, and she wanted it as fiercely as she had ever wanted anything in her life.

'Now I clip your harness to mine,' Tama was saying. 'Like this. And I tell you to put your arms around my neck.'

He was holding her steady. The way he would be holding a patient so that they could both be winched up to a hovering helicopter.

So close Mikki could feel the whole, hard length of Tama's body.

Could feel a strange, humming sensation that went through the layers of clothing and then skin and muscle to settle in her bones with a liquid warmth so exquisite Mikki had to bite her lip to prevent the escape of a soft, appreciative sigh.

Tama stood very still. Silent. For just a heartbeat too long.

Long enough for the undercurrents to be shining like neon lamps.

There was no way out of this unless Mikki could pull back far enough to see Tama's face and then say something. *Anything.* A stupid question about the carabiners linking their harnesses would do the trick. Something that sounded professional enough to diffuse this tension.

Mikki managed the first part of the plan but then the words failed to form and she found herself staring into Tama's eyes and the tension rocketed up. They were so close.

Way too close. When Tama's gaze dropped from her eyes to her lips, she knew he was thinking about kissing her. It was like that moment in the diving pool, with the major difference that they were alone here. No audience. Nobody would know.

No way could Mikki produce a single word now.

Neither could she move enough to even take a new breath. She didn't want to break the spell.

She *wanted* Tama to kiss her.

Any resolutions about avoiding the pull of an attraction that could cost her this career opportunity were relentlessly crushed. There was no way she could resist this man. If he wanted her, she was here. A more than willing partner.

And he did want her. She knew it. Maybe it had always been a matter of 'when', not 'if', and the moment had arrived.

How long had they been like that? Staring at each other? Not long enough for Mikki to feel a desperate need for a new supply of oxygen but it was long enough to feel like for ever.

Long enough to provide a background where the slamming of a side hangar door had all the effect of a gunshot.

Steve had arrived for work and, as the sound of the metal door closing faded away, their pagers sounded.

It hung between them.

That almost kiss.

Like a strand of something solid. A connection Mikki could feel with varying degrees of intensity from that moment on.

So strong to begin with as she climbed into the helicopter with the adrenaline rush of her first callout, having been promoted to second crew member but fading as they arrived at a medical centre an hour's drive from the city where an eleven-year-old was suffering a life threatening asthma attack.

She would not have expected to notice it with the full on effort of keeping this child alive until they reached the hospital. The aggressive drug therapy they instigated was still not enough and in mid-flight the panicked child went into respiratory arrest.

The back of a helicopter had never seemed so cramped or their supplies so awkwardly packed and hard to access. Mikki was at the head of the stretcher, with her arms around their seated patient, her hands on his small rib cage, helping the exhausted boy in his efforts to expel air. Tama was doing his best to secure a second IV line. They both felt the exact moment the child gave up the struggle to breathe and for just a heartbeat the two medics made eye contact with each other.

The boy needed intubation and Mikki couldn't stop herself remembering her failure in a situation that had been this urgent. The first time she had been under Tama's critical evaluation for her clinical skills. They would have to swap positions if Tama was to do this intubation and it would take time they didn't have if they wanted to save this child.

And there was that connection again. Not remotely sexual. It was deeper. Stronger.

It told Mikki that she didn't need to move. That he trusted her. That he was here and would assist but this was something she could do. That she needed to do.

He was right on both counts. Five minutes before they landed on the rooftop helipad of the biggest hospital in town, Mikki had secured the tube that would keep the boy's airway open and she was carefully ventilating him to avoid damaging lungs that were still far from being able to function normally. The paediatric team, including an anaesthetist, was waiting for them in the emergency department and Mikki watched as they adjusted settings on the machine that would take over his breathing, put monitoring lines in place and arranged transfer to the paediatric intensive care unit.

Tama stood beside her and when the admitting team finally nodded their satisfaction at the stability of their patient's condition, Tama looked down and smiled at Mikki and she could feel the strength of that connection all over again.

'Shall we go and visit Josh before we head back to station?'

'Of course.' Concern for their colleague came back in a rush and Mikki realised what an emotional roller-coaster this day was presenting. No wonder she was feeling a little strange.

Vulnerable.

And no wonder the relief of seeing a smile on Josh's face brought tears to her eyes.

'Hey, I'm not dead, Mouse.'

'You could have been. Thank God the wheel went over your foot and not your head.'

'He would have been fine in that case,' Tama growled. 'Not much to damage at that end, is there, mate?'

Laughter chased away the threat of the silly, feminine tears and then something new got thrown into the emotional cauldron of Mikki's day.

Pride.

'You should've seen Mouse on this last run,' Tama told his partner. 'Intubating a kid in respiratory arrest. Mid-air. Have to say, if she wasn't heading for war-torn countries in a few months, your job might not be there to come back to.'

'Hey, I can do a threesome. You wouldn't get rid of me that easily.'

The nurse who had come in to check Josh's IV and the attached self-administered pain relief looked up and grinned.

'Threesome, huh?' She raised an eyebrow at Mikki. 'Lucky you.'

'Yeah.' Mikki returned the grin, still bursting with pride from Tama's praise. Feeling closer to both these men than she ever had to any work colleagues.

She loved this job.

She loved them.

For the first time in her life she was exactly where she wanted to be.

She belonged.

And then she made the mistake of catching Tama's gaze, and that strand of connection was like liquid fire. There was nothing professional about this non-verbal communication. It was purely sexual. There would be no 'threesome', his look told her. This was between the two of them.

The temperature of the room seemed to be rising steadily but Josh was now busy flirting with his nurse and apparently didn't notice.

'I might not get in to see you tomorrow,' Tama told Josh a few minutes later as they prepared to leave. 'Depends on Mouse, of course.'

'What does?' Mikki asked.

'I checked my calendar last night,' Tama said casually. 'And the long-range weather forecast today. If you're keen, we could get dropped on the top of a mountain tomorrow and get your survival training out of the way.'

'So soon?' Mikki wasn't sure she was ready. 'I was expecting to have to wait until there was a group for that.'

Josh was clearly getting a good effect from his pain relief medication. He was grinning broadly. 'You're special,' he told Mikki. 'Tama wants to give you the royal treatment.'

'Oi!' Tama's tone held a distinct reprimand. 'It's your fault my diary's clear, mate. We were supposed to be driving up north so you could be at your mum's birthday party, remember?'

Josh groaned. 'Mum's on her way here instead. She's going to sit in the corner of my room and probably knit me a giant sock to go over my leg. You can't leave me alone listening to those needles clacking, Tama. I'll go crazy.'

Tama grinned. 'So would I. Your mum never gives up trying to tell me it's time I settled down and started making babies. Think I'd rather be making a snow cave with the mouse, thanks.'

Mikki tried to ignore the reference to making babies. 'A snow cave?' she echoed. No. She couldn't ignore it after all. 'We'd be spending the night on the top of a mountain?'

'And another one out in the bush.'

'You could wait,' Josh grumbled. 'I'd like to come as well. Could do with a refresher.'

'Can't wait *that* long,' Tama said decisively. 'What about you, Mouse?'

He wasn't looking at Mikki but the innuendo was blatant.

Dropped into the wilderness and forced to spend

their days and nights together, there was absolutely no doubt that the tension simmering between them would have to be addressed.

Tama was creating this opportunity so did it mean he wanted something to happen? If she didn't want that, now was the time to say so. To make some kind of excuse. A prior engagement that would make it impossible to spend the next couple of days alone with Tama. It might be the sensible thing to do.

Carefully, Mikki took a deep breath. She looked at Josh rather than Tama. 'Sorry, mate, but I can't turn down an offer like that, can I? We'll tell you all about it as soon as we get back.'

Tama was right behind her as she stepped out of the room.

'We'll see about that,' he murmured. 'There may be some aspects of your survival training that you might not want to share with everybody.'

CHAPTER SEVEN

SHE could share *this* with everybody.

If she could find the right words.

Words that could convey the sense of desolation she felt seeing Steve taking the helicopter back to base, leaving Tama and herself standing on a snow-covered slope.

The tiny dot of the aircraft faded into the endless blue sky and Mikki had the weird sensation of looking down from even higher than the helicopter had been. Seeing herself and her sole companion fading to black dots on a pristine white background. Insignificant and then invisible as her mind's eye saw the towering peaks of the mountains behind them, the tussock-covered high country below and then mile after mile—as far as the eye could see—of bush-covered land.

Wilderness. The blanket of greenery might give the impression of soft lines but beneath that canopy was a harsh landscape of steep slopes punctuated by baby rivers that tumbled into ravines. Dense bush that would be impenetrable in many places. Slippery tussock sprouting through puddles of icy snow, and where they were right now knee-deep snow, the chill of which

Mikki could feel pressing on her leather boots like a solid weight.

The silence, when the final chop of the helicopter's rotors had faded to nothing, was as awe-inspiring as the scenery. So deep it seemed almost sacrilege to break it. Not that Tama was sharing Mikki's reverence.

'Nice, huh?' He took a deep breath of the cold air. 'You don't get a view like this every day.'

'No.' Mikki was still trying to take it in. To push back a fear she hadn't expected to be so strong.

'You OK?'

'Yes.' No. What did they think they were doing, putting themselves into such a hostile environment voluntarily? This was crazy!

Mikki finally dragged her gaze from the mind-boggling vastness around them. She turned and found it a comfort to see the figure of another human body, especially one as big and solid as Tama. She raised her gaze and there was a pair of dark eyes behind ski goggles staring back. Lips that showed above the black wool of a balaclava were curved into a smile.

'You just need to trust me, princess,' he said. 'Can you do that?'

She had no choice.

They may have spent yesterday evening sorting supplies and clothing and going over basic survival techniques, but there was no way Mikki could be doing this on her own.

She had to trust Tama.

With her life.

Strangely, it was easy to take that step. The fear she had been so aware of ebbed sharply because the trust was genuine. A part of that connection that was so much stronger than simply attraction.

She didn't even mind him calling her 'princess' because she knew there was respect in their bond. Instead of being demeaning, the title was more like an endearment and *that* notion reminded Mikki that there was more on the agenda here than just her survival training.

Excitement replaced fear. A delicious tingle of anticipation.

'Of course I can,' she told Tama. 'I'm assuming you're keen to get off this mountain alive.'

'You bet.'

'And I'm guessing you've done this before.'

'Once or twice.'

'In this particular location?'

'Absolutely.' Tama looked around them, taking a long moment to stare at the mountain peaks. 'I love it up here,' he added. 'We're on top the world. Free.'

Mikki was looking at him rather than the mountains. Listening to a note in his voice she hadn't heard before. A tone that reverberated and gave her the odd urge to touch him. A moment later she realised why. It had been a piece of personal information, hadn't it?

In all the interaction she'd had so far with this man, nothing as personal as a passion for anything other than his work had been apparent. It was like having a drink offered when she hadn't realised how thirsty she was. A tiny taste and Mikki wanted more. A lot more. She wanted to know what else he loved. *Who* he loved. What did he need to feel 'free' from?

'You're staring at me again.'

'Again?'

'You do it a lot.'

'Do I?' It was time to change the subject. 'I'm just waiting for words of wisdom to spill from your lips, that's all. What's first? Do we get to build a snow cave?'

'No.' Tama seemed to be collecting himself. Focussing on what they were there to do. 'We're going to make a mound rather than a cave. Caves are best for a larger group. A mound is all two of us will need for a night.'

Just the two of them. In close quarters. *All* night. Was it just a lower level of oxygen at this high altitude that was making Mikki notice a slight dizziness?

'The first thing we do is STOP,' Tama said firmly.

'Stop what?' Mikki asked nervously. Her wayward thoughts, maybe?

'S.T.O.P.,' he spelt out. 'It stands for Stop, Think, Observe and Plan. What if Steve hadn't just flown off into the sunset? What if he was lying dead in the mangled helicopter we just crawled out of? And what did we wait for before escaping the wreckage?'

They had been over important considerations of surviving a crash last night.

'We waited until all movement had stopped,' Mikki responded obediently. 'We didn't want to get sliced to bits by rotors that were still in the process of shearing off.'

'Good. What should we do now?'

'Wait until the risk of fire has gone and go back to check that the emergency locator beacon is activated and see if the radio works.'

'And?'

'And we try and retrieve the survival pack, if we didn't already bring it out with us.'

'Right.' Tama was well into teaching mode now. 'Our

ELB isn't working for whatever reason and neither is the radio. What now?'

'We try our cellphones.'

'No coverage here.'

'We should stay close to the wreck, which is going to be a lot more visible than we are. We could try and signal a passing aircraft by using mirrors or flares or making a fire.'

'You *were* paying attention.' Tama nodded approvingly, which sent a ridiculously warm glow through Mikki. 'What else should you be thinking about?'

'Any immediate threats to our safety. The dangers of hypothermia and dehydration.'

'What do we need?'

'Shelter. Water. Fire, if possible.' Mikki was enjoying the challenge. 'I think we need to build a shelter close to the wreck, try and keep warm and conserve energy. And if we're not found by morning, we should try and walk out.'

'Sounds like a plan.' Tama raised an eyebrow. 'What have you left out?'

'The patient? If we'd had a patient on board and got them out we wouldn't be able to go anywhere.'

Tama shook his head. 'Keep thinking. Remember STOP.'

'I'm up to P. Oh-h.' Mikki rolled her eyes. 'I haven't observed much, have I?'

'What should we look at?'

'The weather. Terrain. Materials that might be useful.'

'Cool. We know the weather's OK but if this was for real, what might we be looking for?'

'Wind direction and speed. Say, a nor'westerly that

means bad weather's on the way. Strong winds and rain could increase avalanche risk.' Mikki had begun moving her feet without realising it because they were getting cold enough to be painful.

Tama noticed. 'We'll start moving,' he decided. 'You can tell me about the terrain and where any danger areas for avalanche might be if you spot them.'

'Don't we need to plan our route first?'

'We'll talk about that, too.' Tama picked up the small backpack that contained their survival kit. 'I've done this before and our route is carefully planned to give us practice in the skills we need. Follow my steps to start with and watch how I'm kicking the snow to pack it down and then testing it before I put any weight down.' He grinned. 'Should keep us from falling into a crevasse, hopefully. You'll get a turn at keeping us alive later.'

Mikki picked up her pack that held water and dehydrated food and followed Tama. Yes, they would talk about what she was here to learn but it was inevitable that they would talk about other things, wasn't it?

Personal things that might allow her an insight into this intriguing man.

For the next two hours, anyone observing them would have considered themselves simply watching an intense teaching session. Mikki learned how to walk safely on a snow-covered slope. How to examine the terrain around, above and below them and how to describe a col and a gully and a buttress.

She learned how to spot changes in the snow that might indicate a hazard and how to estimate distances and plan a route that might eventually lead to safety. She spent some time choosing the place to build their shelter for the night and then they started the task that Tama said would take them another couple of hours.

The undercurrent—of being completely isolated with that simmering, as yet unexplored, physical attraction between her and Tama was just that. An unacknowledged undercurrent that was there with every burst of conversation and every shared glance. A pleasant sensation that suggested they were both going with the flow rather than fighting it.

A new depth was being added to their relationship, Mikki realised. Amidst the energy that came from a skilled teacher interacting with a willing student she could sense more than Tama's passion for his subject. There was a palpable pride in what he did. Who he was. Real patience in leading her to teach herself what she needed to know and a genuine interest in her success.

In *her*?

They took turns with the small shovel from Tama's pack to heap snow into a large mound. Tama took over when the height was above Mikki's head level. He made the task look easy and didn't even get particularly out of breath while he talked at the same time. He told her the story of a plane-crash victim who survived against huge odds and walked out of the bush a week later, mid-winter, in nothing more than a pair of shorts and a T-shirt.

'Sometimes,' he concluded, 'I think survival is more about sheer bloody-mindedness and refusing to give up than all the fancy stuff we can teach. Have you got that kind of determination, Mikki?'

He'd called her 'Mikki'. Not 'princess' or 'Mouse'. This was new. And it was a personal question. Was

Tama feeling the same kind of curiosity about her that she was about him?

'I guess,' she responded carefully. 'I'm here, aren't I? Given how over-protective my dad is, it's taken a fair bit of determination to get this far.'

Tama seemed to be shovelling harder. 'We need to get a good dome shape to this,' he said. 'That way we can maintain an arch shape when we hollow it out. That makes the roof self-supporting and it won't drip on us.' He threw another shovelful of snow upwards. 'Why is your father so over-protective?'

'My mother died just before my tenth birthday. Dad absolutely adored her and her death very nearly destroyed him. For a while, he pushed me away totally but…when he found he was able to love again, he went a bit too far the other way. Wanted to wrap me up in cotton wool and make sure he didn't lose someone else, I suppose.'

'You're an only child?'

'Yes. Mum was diagnosed with breast cancer at the same appointment she found out she was pregnant with me.'

The movement of the shovel ceased. 'Wow. That must have been tough. Did she put off treatment?'

'Yes.' Mikki had to turn and pretend she was admiring the scenery again. Boy, Tama knew how to get straight to the heart of a painful subject, didn't he? Had she really wanted to start treading on personal ground like this?

The silence continued. Respectful. Waiting.

'I didn't know that until after she died,' Mikki said finally. 'Some well-meaning friend was trying to find a way to help Dad with his depression and I overheard her talking to another friend. She thought he might be blaming himself because he allowed her to continue with the pregnancy instead of starting chemo.'

Another silence fell in which Mikki could feel Tama staring at her.

'So you blamed yourself instead.'

Mikki turned swiftly. 'Why did you say that?'

'It's what kids do.' It was too hard to see Tama's eyes behind the ski goggles from this distance but she could see sympathy in every line of his face. 'Their world gets tipped upside down and someone they love gets ripped away from them. We're egocentric creatures at the best of times and when you're too young to know any better, or there's no one around who knows or cares how you feel and you don't get told it's not true, it's inevitable you end up thinking it's your fault.'

The words were heartfelt. So heartfelt it was Mikki's turn to stare intently at Tama.

She had to clear her throat to break the new silence. 'What did you blame yourself for, Tama?'

Tama dug the shovel into the snow forcefully and heaved the load upwards, grateful for a physically demanding task.

Dammit. That had been unbelievably careless. But how had Mikki picked up that he was talking about himself so easily? It was like she could see the part of him he'd been able to keep so well hidden for so many years.

'I'm just saying,' he muttered. 'That's what kids are like.'

He needed to direct the conversation back to safe

ground. Why had he asked such a personal question in the first place? He knew perfectly well what level of determination this pint-sized woman possessed.

This had been a mistake. He'd got carried away back there when they'd been visiting Josh. Pushed the boundaries of the game thanks to the temptation that nurse's comment had provoked. A threesome? No way. But the idea of being alone—just him and Mikki—had been irresistible. And so easy to arrange with no suspicions being raised.

But it had been a mistake. He needed to back off and get this excursion onto purely professional grounds.

'We can start digging the tunnel now.' Tama stepped away from the impressively large mound of snow. 'We start out here and go down about a metre. We won't come up until we're well under the edge of the mound and then we'll start hollowing out from the middle. I'll shovel it behind me and you can scoop it up and get rid of it.'

The task was not difficult but it was time-consuming and they had to rest at intervals to conserve energy.

Verbal interaction was minimal because Mikki was out of sight and busy behind him. When there was an opportunity to say something, Tama kept right away from anything personal. He had a wealth of stories he could tell about how people dealt with survival in the wilderness. Plus any number of useful tips.

'Don't ever carry a butane lighter with your survival kit,' he warned Mikki. 'Too damn dangerous. Have an airtight, melt-proof container and keep waterproof matches or magnesium fire-starters in it.

'Use your watch for a compass. Keep it flat and point

the hour hand at the sun. Half the distance between the hour hand and twelve o'clock is due south.

'You can make a decent fishing hook by bending a syringe needle. I'll show you tomorrow when we get near the river.'

It worked for a while, even though it felt forced at best and a bit ridiculous at times. It wasn't so easy to control his thoughts while he was alone in the centre of the mound, carving out the space they would share for the night. He kept thinking about the kind of darkness her words had skimmed. A darkness he could understand only too well.

Was that where her astonishing strength of character came from? That period of heading into adolescence, not only missing the person she needed most. But carrying the burden of guilt that her very existence might have contributed to her mother's death?

He gave up trying to squash his curiosity when he emerged to share a drink of water and a muesli bar from Mikki's pack.

'At least your dad didn't blame you,' he found himself saying out of the blue. 'Or he wouldn't have been so over-protective.'

'That came later,' Mikki said. 'After the car accident when I was sixteen.'

Ah, yes. That accident. He'd been curious about that when she'd mentioned it the day of that physical assessment. It had been so easy to stay away from stepping onto personal ground back then. Not so easy now.

'You were hurt?' The mental image of Mikki lying badly injured in the kind of scenes he often attended was disturbing enough to give him a kick in the gut.

'Amazingly, no, but the other three teenagers in the

car were hurt. One of them died. I was the front-seat passenger and…I got lucky, I guess.'

'They were your friends?'

'Yeah…' She didn't sound sure.

'A boyfriend was one of them?'

'No.' Mikki's tone told him it was time to stop prying. Clearly, she didn't want to talk about it.

That was fine. Good, even. They could really get away from this personal stuff. He could dismiss his curiosity about those intervening years. The ones between her mother's death and the accident that had made her father so over-protective. Had he not cared much until then? Been so focussed on a sick wife and then too broken-hearted to really notice his kid? She must have been incredibly lonely if that had been the case. Not that he was going to ask but he didn't like the idea of her being a lonely child any more than being injured.

Mikki broke into his thoughts. 'What about you?' she asked. 'Were you an only child?'

Maybe they couldn't stay away from this personal stuff after all. He'd brought this on himself, though, hadn't he?

'Yes and no,' Tama answered reluctantly. He pushed the top of his water bottle shut with a snap, shoved it back into the pack and turned to climb back into the tunnel. Then he caught Mikki watching him and sighed inwardly.

'Yeah, OK. It's just not something I tell people.' *Ever.* So why did it feel like the time to break that ironclad rule? Because Mikki had experienced something that might give her insight into how it had really been? There was something there. A connection. A kind of force that pulled the words from his mouth. 'Yes, I was an only child. I didn't have a dad that I knew about. I got sent to live with my uncle and aunt and eleven cousins.'

Tama ducked his head into the tunnel. He'd said enough. Too much.

Mikki's voice floated into the tunnel with him. 'How old were you?'

'About six,' Tama growled. He wriggled further into the mound. This conversation was over.

Mikki crouched at the neck of the tunnel, ready to scoop the snow that came towards her and spread it away from the opening.

She had barely heard Tama's muttered response to her question but it resonated in her head as loudly as if he'd shouted it.

He'd been six. A small child.

For whatever reason, his mother had given him up and sent him to live with relatives. To be one of a huge family where one more mouth to feed probably hadn't been noticed. *He* might not have been noticed.

Just like her, he'd lost his mother.

And he'd blamed himself, hadn't he? That was why those words had been so heartfelt.

As a little boy, Tama had felt unloved and possibly very lonely, and he'd believed it was his own fault. That somehow, unknowingly, he'd done something so wrong he'd had to be severely punished.

Mikki's heart ached. For Tama. For herself. For the children they had been and for what had been taken from them. No wonder she felt so drawn to this man. Was it the similarity of their pasts that attracted them both to this kind of work? This unique combination of risking yourself to care for others?

Was the reason she felt Tama was a soulmate as simple as that?

Maybe.

Except that there was another factor in this attraction.

A very physical one.

The inside of the snow mound had a wide platform against one side and a narrower one against the other.

'We sleep there,' Tama explained, pointing to the wider platform. 'And we cook on this one.'

'Cook?'

'Didn't I tell you I can cook?' Tama was using a tiny bright light that was remarkably effective in the confines of this small space. 'Watch this.'

He produced a tiny primus stove from his pack and a small, lightweight, aluminium pan. Mikki found the water and the packages of dehydrated food he requested and then did as instructed and watched, increasingly aware of how intimate this situation was.

Here they were, in a tiny cocoon, so isolated that the rest of the world might as well have ceased to exist.

Just herself and Tama. In a space small enough to be warmed by the combination of their body heat and the small stove. When an absolutely delicious smell began to emanate from the pan, it felt—ridiculously—like home.

Mikki cast an anxious glance upwards a moment later, however.

'Won't the heat from the flames melt the roof?'

'A bit, but it won't drip on us. That's the beauty of

making a good arch shape. It won't cave in either, so don't worry.'

Mikki smiled. 'I'm so hungry I don't care. It would be worth it.'

They both had a spoon and they took turns eating the hot mixture of pasta, meat and vegetables. A muesli bar stuffed with chocolate chips was dessert.

'Still hungry?' Tama asked as Mikki washed down her last mouthful with a swig of water.

'No. And I'm heaps warmer. I feel great.'

The warmth from Tama's approving gaze made her feel even better. Mikki liked it that they didn't need to wear the goggles in here. She loved being able to see Tama's eyes. To try and read his expressions. She just wished she knew more of what was going on behind those dark eyes. Maybe she was still hungry. Just not for food.

'I'm warm, too,' Tama said. 'Amazingly effective shelter, isn't it? Put your gloves back on, though. We don't want to risk frostbite while we sleep.'

Mikki pulled on woollen gloves and then her waterproof, thermal mittens as Tama opened a small package that contained a foil sheet. He spread it on the sleeping platform as she pulled her woollen hat on more securely and made sure her anorak was zipped up. She stepped into the sleeping bag Tama handed her from the pack and pulled it up to her waist.

'I'm going to turn off the light,' Tama warned. 'Come and make yourself comfortable on the bed.'

A bed they were about to share. Mikki's mouth felt dry and she had to lick her lips. Did Tama feel this sudden tension? Should she try and make it go away by making a joke?

'Hey.' She grinned, hopping a step closer. 'I'm not sure we know each other well enough to sleep together yet.'

The only response to her remark was to be plunged into total darkness as Tama flicked off the light. Then, out of the darkness and silence, came Tama's voice. A low rumble that made Mikki's toes curl inside her heavy boots.

'We know each other just fine,' he said.

CHAPTER EIGHT

'YOU'RE perfectly safe.'

Tama sat down on the snow platform and then lay down, his head going behind Mikki's back as she stayed sitting on the edge. His tone was amused.

'We'd be risking hypothermia taking any of our clothes off. Lie down, Mouse. You must be tired.'

She was and she did. Cautiously. It was hard to share this space without touching the body of the large man lying beside her, but they were so padded up in their multiple layers of protective clothing, it didn't really matter.

It shouldn't matter anyway. But, then, she shouldn't be able to sense the heat from his body like this. To feel his touch through all those layers as clearly as if he was touching her skin.

Mikki moved a moment later, uncomfortably aware of the pressure of Tama's hip against hers.

'Be still,' Tama murmured.

Mikki froze instantly. The words transported her back to that day in the diving pool when he'd just pulled her from the helicopter 'wreck' and she was taking that long-awaited breath of air. She could see his face so close to her own. Could feel that first rush of desire to touch his lips with her own.

Oh, *help*! Her cringe was almost a wriggle.

'What's up?' Tama asked. 'You cold?'

'Nope. I'm good.'

'Could've fooled me.'

'This is just a bit…weird.'

It was automatic to turn her head towards the person she was talking to. Not that she could see Tama. This was a darkness like nothing she had ever experienced. She wouldn't be able to see her hand if she held it close enough to touch her nose.

Funny how it heightened other senses. She could feel Tama's breath on her face. *Smell* him. A musky, masculine scent she could almost taste.

'Scared, huh?'

Mikki hesitated. 'Yes.' The admission was reluctant because she wouldn't be surprised if Tama thought less of her for it, but it was the truth. There was a real element of fear still lurking. If Tama hadn't been here beside her, she would be terrified.

'You should be,' Tama said quietly. 'Any intelligent person would be in a situation like this.' He was shifting his weight now. Putting his arm around Mikki and pulling her closer. 'You're OK,' he said. 'I'm here.'

Mikki absorbed the reassurance. Allowed herself to sink into the circle of his arm and let the side of her body mould itself to his. Maybe she didn't need to be so afraid of their environment but she still didn't feel safe being this close to Tama.

'It still feels weird,' she said into the new silence.

'Why?' Tama chuckled and the puff of breath was warm. 'You don't make a habit of sleeping with men in holes in the snow?'

The teasing diffused the tension. 'I don't make a habit of sleeping with men at all.'

'Whoa!' She could hear Tama suck in his breath. 'You a virgin, princess?'

'No.' For some obscure reason it felt like an insult. As though she might not be attractive enough to have had the opportunity. Or too uptight to consider sex before marriage acceptable. 'And don't call me that.'

'Why not?'

'I don't like it.'

'Hmm.' Tama sounded interested now. 'What else don't you like? Apart from sleeping with men, that is.'

Mikki wanted to hit him. 'I didn't say I didn't *like* sleeping with men. I said I didn't make a *habit* of it.'

'Good. Delighted to hear it.'

He sounded delighted. Why? What business was it of his, anyway?

'What about you?' Mikki countered.

'I *never* sleep with men.'

Mikki snorted. 'Very funny.'

'And you're the first woman I've slept with in…oh, ages.'

'Yeah, weeks, I bet. And you're not *sleeping* with me.'

'Not yet,' Tama conceded graciously. 'But I will.'

Mikki held her breath unconsciously. There was such promise in those few words but did he mean slumber or sex?

'You're not breathing,' Tama said softly.

'Yes, I am.' Mikki let her breath out with a whoosh. 'See?'

'Just as well. I was just starting to think I might need to resuscitate you.'

Mouth-to-mouth resuscitation? Mikki swallowed. She hadn't imagined that tone of disappointment beneath the light banter. Was he looking for an excuse to kiss her? Desire kicked in and her heart missed a beat and sped up. It felt so obvious she was afraid Tama would be able to feel it as well. She tried to slow her heart rate by slowing her breathing. But that made it very quiet.

'Uh-oh,' Tama murmured. 'You're doing it again.'

He was so close Mikki could feel the words as much as hear them, and the distance closed as he spoke so that by the time he spoke the last word it simply morphed into a kiss. The talking finished but his lips kept moving on top of hers. Gently. And then more firmly.

It was a conversation all of its own with all the nuances that speech could contain with the tiny variations of pressure and position. Despite the deafening level of sound desire was trying to make, Mikki could 'hear' the underlying communication.

I like you. I'm interested.

Me, too.

I like this. Do you?

Yes. Oh…yes!

The kiss went on. And on. Desire was tightly reined in, which made it possible for this conversation to seem relaxed. A pleasure in itself that was not necessarily leading to anything else.

As naturally as the verbal communication had become non-verbal, the process was reversed.

'Nice,' Tama murmured as he drew back slowly. 'Very nice.'

'Mmm.' Mikki ran her tongue over her lower lip. It still tingled. It still tasted of Tama. 'Nice' was far too pale a word.

'You're still safe,' Tama told her. 'I don't do relationships.'

'Oh?' The statement should have been reassuring. Where did that frisson of disappointment come from?

'No.' The affirmation was definite.

'How old are you?'

'Thirty-six.'

'And you've never had a relationship?'

'Define "relationship".'

'Um…' Mikki had to think. 'If you see someone more than a couple of times it becomes a relationship because you have the expectation of seeing them again. You *want* to see them again.'

'Does it involve sex?'

'At some point, if it's an adult relationship, then sex is involved. That's what makes it a relationship rather than just a friendship.'

'OK. In that case, I take it back. I've had heaps of relationships.'

'If you go into it knowing that it's short term, it's not a *real* relationship,' Mikki continued as she thought aloud. 'It becomes real when you start caring about that person. When you have the expectation that it's going to continue and lead to something else.'

'Like marriage and mortgages?'

'I guess.'

'Then no. I was right. I've never had a real relationship

and I don't intend to. Any hint that a woman wants that stuff and I'm outta there. Not my scene. How 'bout you?'

'It's not something I can see in my immediate future,' Mikki said confidently. 'But I wouldn't say "never". Maybe, one day, when I meet the right person, I'll change my mind.'

'Really?'

'Sure. Why not?'

'Because you've seen what it can do to someone.'

'What do you mean?'

'You said it nearly destroyed your father when your mother died. He must have loved her very much. They must have had the best kind of relationship.'

'They did. And, yes, he adored her.'

'And it was nearly the end of the world for him when he lost her. It must have been unbearable. I've seen that happen, too. Why put yourself at risk like that?'

'Because…' Mikki was getting an insight into herself through Tama that she'd never considered. Was she the same? Had she run from any relationship that looked like it was getting serious because she didn't want to risk the fallout if things went wrong? 'It must be worth it. It's that "better to have loved and lost" theory.'

'I don't buy into it,' Tama said dismissively. 'There's other good stuff to be found in life. Like this…'

He was kissing her again. And this time it felt even more natural than the first time. His taste was familiar and…wonderful. His warmth seeped into every cell in Mikki's body and the movement of his lips sent impulses that brought her whole body alive. Made it tingle with energy and contentment and desire all at the same time.

And then his tongue touched hers and Mikki lost any

ability to analyse how she felt. The world had already been banished to this tiny space and now her awareness shrank much further. She just existed in that point of contact between herself and Tama. A white-hot flame that flickered and grew and consumed everything else. Including oxygen. Mikki finally had to pull back to drag in a breath of air.

'This isn't good.'

'What?' Tama sounded astonished. 'I thought it was pretty fantastic myself. Best kiss I've had in…oh, ages.'

Mikki suppressed a smile. 'I meant it's not a good idea. We can't have sex, Tama.'

'No. That would require a little less in the way of clothing than we currently have and it would be silly to risk dying of hypothermia.'

'I meant not at all.'

'We're only kissing.'

'And kissing is generally the first step on a path that leads to a lot more.' It would be too disappointing to get more of Tama's kisses and know they were leading to nothing more. Better to pull the plug right now. 'What happens when we're not sleeping on top of a mountain? Tomorrow, say, or next week?'

'Do you want a lot more, Mouse?'

'No.' *Yes.*

'You sure about that?' Tama's lips were teasing hers again.

'We *can't*.' Mikki was desperately trying to remember why it was such a bad idea. Oh, yes… 'It would be… completely inappropriate.'

'Would it?'

'Yes. Of course it would. You must see that.'

'Help me out here. We're both adults, aren't we?'

'Y-yes.'

'And we're both single. At least, I'm single. How 'bout you?'

'Of course I'm single. I wouldn't be kissing you if I wasn't.'

'I also get the impression that neither of us is into those long-term, *real* relationships you were talking about. Not yet, in your case, anyway.' A hint of alarm crept into his voice. 'You don't see me as husband material do you?'

Mikki almost laughed. 'No way! And I'm certainly not looking. Settling down anywhere—with *anyone*— is the last thing I want right now. I've got way too much to do with my life first.'

'So there you go. We're the same, you and me.' Tama's grip on Mikki tightened by way of emphasis. 'We want the same things. So why not sex? I think…' Tama's lips touched Mikki's again and his tongue stroked hers for just a heartbeat. 'I think it would be very, *very* good.'

Mikki had absolutely no doubts about that.

'You're my teacher.' She forced the words out in a rush. 'I'm with you because I need to learn stuff.'

'Agreed.' She could hear Tama smiling. 'So the curriculum has some extras. I'm sure there's some things I could teach you in bed, princess.'

Oh, *Lord*! Mikki had absolutely no doubts about *that* either.

'I'm dependent on you for a qualification I really want to get, Tama. That makes it inappropriate. Unethical. If anyone knew, you'd get into big trouble. I'd

probably end up having to leave without the qualifications I need to get me into MSF.'

'What if it didn't? What if nobody knew about it
except us?'

'It's way too risky. What if it turned to custard and
you took your revenge by failing me?'

'It wouldn't.'

'Why not?'

'Because we're not talking *real* here, that's why not.
We're talking sexual attraction. At least, that's what it
is for me. I know it's inappropriate and I've tried to ignore it, but it doesn't seem to be going away. Quite the
opposite.' He sighed, an eloquent admission of defeat,
and when he spoke again, his voice was husky. 'I want
you.' His lips were close to Mikki's again and she felt
his words right through her body. 'And I think…' He
paused to brush her lips very softly. 'I think you might
feel the same way.'

'Mmm.' The sound was strangled. Embarrassingly
close to a moan, really.

'So maybe we should just get it out of our systems.
Deal with it. Unresolved sexual tension could lead to
frustration that might interfere more with your training
than your imagined fallout that's not going to happen
because we're not going to have a *real* relationship. We
can't, can we? You're not even going to be around for
long enough.'

'That's true. A couple of months at the most, if you
do your job properly.'

'So there you go. We're talking a few weeks. We don't
even need to think that far ahead. This could be a one-off
situation. A kind of debrief. A way of defusing tension.'

'A one-off?' Mikki didn't like that idea. It was too casual. Cheap.

'Theoretically. I guess what I'm saying here is that we shouldn't take it too seriously. We know what we want and there's no real reason why we shouldn't go there and then take it one step at a time. See what happens. I reckon we could make it work.'

'And nobody would find out?'

'Not from me, they wouldn't.'

'And you wouldn't let it interfere with work? With my training?'

'That would be unethical. I'm not an unethical person, Mikki, I promise you that.'

He'd used her name again.

And he'd made a promise she knew instinctively she could trust. Just like she was trusting him to get her through this survival training.

'Think about it,' Tama said. He let his breath out in a sigh and pulled her even closer. 'Right now, we should sleep. We've got a big day tomorrow.'

Think about it, he'd said.

He'd meant for Mikki to think about it, but in the bright light of the new day, it was all Tama could think about himself. He'd dreamt about it, with his arm holding Mikki's body against his while he'd slept.

He'd wanted to kiss her the moment he'd opened his eyes to find her still snuggled against him. He'd wanted to breathe warmth into her body in case she was as chilled and stiff as he felt.

Instead, he'd made breakfast. Hot porridge and strong coffee. And he'd talked about the programme for the second day of training. How they would leave the snow and head for a river crossing and into the bush. How she would learn to make a shelter from brushwood and a fire from scratch.

He didn't mention a thing about that intimate conversation in the dark. The ball was in Mikki's court and it would be her choice whether she picked it up or not. However badly Tama wanted it, he wasn't going to influence her decision. If she was going to come to him, she had to want to.

If this was going to work, she had to want him as badly as he wanted her. And the ground rules had to be sacrosanct.

He hadn't said a word.

All day.

Either he'd lost interest or he was leaving the decision entirely up to her.

Mikki thought about those kisses and knew he wouldn't have lost interest any more than she had. She liked it that he wasn't putting any pressure on her. That he was giving her the choice. But it also made her feel curiously shy.

To come right out and say that, yes, she'd given it some thought and decided it was a great idea seemed way too brazen. She couldn't think of a way to say it with just the right degree of lightness so she ended up saying nothing about it at all. Just like Tama.

She listened to her mentor and asked questions about what he was teaching her, and she followed him and did everything she was instructed to do.

They worked their way carefully down a slope with

patches of icy snow between clumps of tussock. They chose a safe crossing place for the baby river and Mikki crossed her arms and held hands with Tama to give them greater weight and stability as they negotiated the shallow but fast-moving water.

They pushed their way into the bush and Mikki learned about which plants were edible and which were poisonous. They discussed the effects of Giardia parasites and how to treat water to make it safe to drink.

As promised, Tama showed her how to make a fishing hook and line when they came across the larger river they would follow downstream, but they didn't try their luck fishing for long.

'We've got enough food for tonight and there's a fair way to walk yet. You tired?'

'A bit,' Mikki admitted. 'It'll be nice to stop.' She was tired of walking with wet and squelchy boots and she was tired of trying to interpret every glance or touch from Tama to gauge what he might be thinking. Whether what had happened between them last night was on his mind as much as it was on hers.

But even when they stopped walking, she couldn't find a way of steering the conversation to anything really personal. It was far easier to stick with the teaching session and learn how to gather brushwood and join it together to make a shelter. How to find small twigs for kindling and then to light the fire by using a magnesium fire-starter.

'Shave pieces off one side with your pocket knife,' Tama instructed. 'And then you make a spark using that piece of flint embedded in the other side.'

Hot food, as daylight faded, was again very welcome.

The warmth from the fire was wonderful but Mikki eyed the narrow space beneath the shelter she had constructed dubiously.

'It's still going to be cold tonight, isn't it?'

'Yep. Usually is, outside like this.'

Too cold to take their clothes off, then. Mikki's nod was resigned but her heart rate picked up. If she was going to say anything, this was her chance. She swallowed. Then she cleared her throat. 'It would be silly to risk hypothermia.'

'It would.' But Tama was smiling. He was reading the direction of her thoughts easily and his smile was enough to give her a lot more courage.

'Shame,' she murmured.

They sat in silence for a minute.

'There *is* a hut,' Tama said.

'What?'

'I told you this route was carefully chosen. There's a hut about half a mile away. We needed one available as a precaution, in case someone got injured on a training exercise or the weather turned nasty. It's got a clearing beside it which is where the chopper's going to pick us up first thing in the morning.'

'So why are we out here instead of in a nice, warm hut?'

'Because it's part of the training. You needed to learn to make a shelter.'

'I've done that.'

Tama glanced over his shoulder. 'So you have.'

'If we happened to be near the clearing a little earlier than expected, no one would need to know why, would they?'

'No.'

'But…' Mikki felt embarrassed now. 'It still wouldn't be a good idea to…you know…'

'Have sex?' Tama supplied helpfully.

'Mmm.'

'Why not? We wouldn't be risking discovery. Or hypothermia.'

'We might be risking something else.'

'We've agreed on the ground rules. It's not going to interfere with your training and it's not going to get messed up by one of us being stupid enough to think it's real.'

'That's not what I meant. I'm talking about…' Mikki closed her eyes. This was horribly clinical. 'You know. Safe sex.'

'Oh-h. Not a problem.'

Mikki's eyes snapped open. 'You're telling me you carry condoms on a survival training exercise?'

Tama's grin was unrepentant. 'I'm a good Boy Scout. Always prepared. But, no, I don't *always* carry them. This time I did.'

Mikki opened her mouth, ready to express outrage at the implied expectation, but then she shut it again. She thought back to that moment in Josh's room. That silent acknowledgement that had passed between them of the attraction and the opportunity that being alone together would provide.

She stood up. 'Seeing as you're such a good Boy Scout,' she said, with a very womanly smile. 'You'll know what to do to make this fire safe to leave, won't you?'

They held hands as they stumbled along a rough track that led to a primitive but sturdy wooden hut. There was a pot-belly stove opposite the door that made the interior deliciously warm in a very short period of time. They both took off their outer, waterproof garments and their balaclavas and gloves and boots.

Leaving the door of the stove open provided a warm, glowing light. Enough to illuminate the narrow bunk beds built into both sides of the hut. Mikki looked at the width of the beds. She looked at the size of Tama and then she looked at the door.

'There's no chance anyone else will want to use this hut tonight, is there?'

'If they did, they would have been here before nightfall, and that was quite a while ago now.'

'Good.'

Mikki pulled a mattress off a bunk and put it on the floor in front of where Tama was stoking up the stove. She added a second mattress beside it and the whole floor area was virtually covered.

It was such an obvious move that Mikki felt embarrassed having completed it. She couldn't look at Tama because the courage she'd found to let him know what she wanted had deserted her. Setting up bedding like this made her feel suddenly and horribly…cheap.

It took only a small step for Tama to be close enough to touch her. He put his forefinger under her chin and used just enough pressure to make her lift her face and look up at him.

She saw understanding in his gaze. Reassurance. And then he smiled that gorgeous crooked smile and bent his head to claim her lips with his own.

* * *

They shouldn't be doing this.

Tama knew that, despite the arguments to the contrary he'd presented to Mikki last night.

He also knew he couldn't have continued resisting the temptation without repercussions. He'd been honest when he'd said that sexual frustration could interfere with their professional relationship more than any aftermath was likely to.

Mikki held her arms up like a child as he helped her undress by pulling the tight thermal top from her body, but there was nothing childlike about the way she dropped her arms around his neck and then stood on tiptoe to offer him her mouth.

Tama let his lips savour hers while his hands unclipped her bra and then slid slowly forward to trace her ribs and find…

Oh, *God*! He might have denied it so well he'd believed it but he'd been wanting to touch these small, perfect breasts since he'd first clapped eyes on them by the diving pool that day. He'd known how they would fit his hands. How firm and round they would feel. He hadn't imagined what it would do to him to feel the tiny, hard nub of an aroused nipple on them, though. With a groan he had to abandon the sweetness of Mikki's mouth and bend lower to explore with his tongue the place he'd just sensitised with his fingers.

Any thoughts of how wrong some might see this as being went up in smoke along with the crackle of the logs in the pot-belly stove. Thoughts like he might be abusing a position of power. Using Mikki simply for his own pleasure.

No. The sounds she was making as he slipped his hands inside her pants to help her undress further made it quite clear that Mikki was getting just as much pleasure from this as he was.

Maybe she was using *him*.

Tama stripped off his own clothes and, for a long moment, he looked at Mikki. Standing naked in the glow from the fire. She was tiny and vulnerable and…the most beautiful woman he'd ever seen. He would have to be so careful not to hurt her.

'You're lovely, Mikki,' he said quietly. 'Just…perfect.'

She raised her gaze from where she had been returning the visual exploration.

'You're not so bad yourself.'

Striving to sound casual might have worked except for that tell-tale wobble in her voice that spoke of barely restrained passion. Her gaze was steady, however. Mikki knew what she was doing there and she knew what she wanted.

Whatever the motivation for this, it was mutual. They both wanted it badly and if you wanted something enough you made sure it worked. Who had he been trying to kid by suggesting that this was going to be a one-off experience?

Tama drew Mikki close. Skin to skin. He kissed her until her legs were as wobbly as her voice had been and then he let his own knees bend, controlling their fall until they were cushioned on the mattresses and Mikki was lying beneath him. Reaching for him. Ready to take him to the place he most wanted to be.

Tama made sure he took Mikki with him to that place but later, much later, as he finally eased far enough away to find the clothing and sleeping bags they would need for the rest of the night, he had to seek reassurance.

'OK, babe?'

'I'm good.'

'What do you reckon?' Tama tried to keep the question light—as though a negative response would be perfectly acceptable. As though he wasn't already planning a way of getting more of the paradise he'd just discovered. 'We got it out of our systems?'

There was a short silence.

'No,' Mikki said decisively. 'Not quite yet.'

CHAPTER NINE

TAMA JAMES was clearly a man of his word.

He'd said nobody would find out and even when they went to visit his best friend together the day after they returned, he didn't do or say anything that could have raised suspicion from Josh.

'How was it?' Josh asked Mikki. 'Did you find it hard? Scary? Exciting?'

'All of the above,' she responded, careful not to look in Tama's direction.

'Did she pass?' Josh asked Tama.

'I reckon.'

Mikki stole a glance but Tama wasn't looking her way either.

'I survived two nights in the wild with Tama,' she told Josh with a grin. 'I reckon I can survive anything.'

'So true.' Josh nodded. 'Hey, I passed my consultant's visit this morning. Neurology in my foot's fine. They're talking about letting me out by the end of next week. I told Mum I'd go home for a week or two to recuperate. It was the only way I could stop her setting up camp in this room.'

'By the end of next week,' Mikki said, 'I might pass my winch training.'

'Whoa!' Tama was looking at her for the first time since they'd arrived for this visit. Sternly. 'Don't go jumping the gun, princess. It's me that gets to decide that stuff.'

'So decide,' Josh said. 'I told you ages ago that Mikki was ready to start winch training.'

Mikki nodded. 'I could get frustrated,' she said demurely. 'It wouldn't be good for our professional relationship.'

Tama was glaring at her now but it was a cover-up. Mikki could detect a lurking twinkle. 'We'll see,' was all he said.

Nobody at work guessed anything either.

It helped that Alistair was on station as the replacement crew member. Because he was new to the station and the crew, it bumped up Mikki's position from being the latest addition. A degree of familiarity and an enjoyment of her colleague's company was perfectly acceptable, and no eyebrows were raised if they let something slip about being together out of hours because Mikki took up a casual membership at the gym complex Tama used. The same one where she'd done her physical prerequisite. Friendly rivalry over fitness regimes became part of the daily conversation on station.

'So who won last night?' Alistair would ask.

'Me,' Mikki might say. 'I was half a length ahead when we finished twenty lengths of the pool.'

And she could smile at Tama. Take just a moment to bask in the eye contact. To hug the knowledge that there had been no winners or losers later that night. That while their physical competition in the gym was fierce, in bed there was gentleness. A desire to give pleasure that seemed limitless so far in its ability to grow and deliver. While they'd only had a single night together in Tama's apartment that first week back, they'd had two nights this week and she knew they were both wondering how long they would have to wait for their next out-of-hours encounter. How many nights together in a week would they be having by the end of the month?

The idea that they would get this attraction out of their systems by acting on it had become a private joke. An excuse to spend more and more time together. And it was working. Just like Tama had promised it could. As long as Mikki didn't let herself get in too deep. As long as she didn't make the mistake of thinking it meant more than it did.

She was safe enough. She'd never fallen in love to the extent that being with a man was more important than the goals she had set herself in life, and Tama had made it very clear how he felt on the subject, so it simply wasn't going to happen. And if things started to look like they were getting out of hand, the limited timeframe they had available was the best insurance policy either of them could have asked for.

No one questioned how much time Tama and Mikki spent together during any downtime on station because it was all professional. Tama had given in to Mikki's relentless pressure and had begun her winch training in earnest, and winch training was time-consuming.

For Mikki, it was easy to keep it professional because there was so much to learn and it was all so exciting. By the end of the second week back after the survival training, she had completed all her on-ground training. She could describe, identify and explain the use of all the components and pieces of equipment to be used and do all the safety checks. She could demonstrate knowledge of the winch and its operation. She had absorbed all the written and audiovisual material available and had learned the protocols and the vocabulary for communication. On the last day, when the shift ended and there was no danger of being called out, she was ready to do her ten-metre work in the safety of the hangar.

The station manager had given his approval.

'But be careful,' he told Tama. A look passed between Andy and Tama that Mikki couldn't read. 'Keep it supersafe.'

'Of course.'

'Don't do anything you don't feel confident about,' Andy told Mikki. 'You don't need to rush this. You could leave it a while yet, you know. Why don't you take the copilot seat for any winch missions that come up from now on. You'd get practical demonstrations that'd be a good learning experience and you wouldn't get left behind on station.'

'I want to do this,' Mikki assured him.

'She's getting frustrated,' Tama added.

'Oh.' Andy looked from Mikki to Tama and back again. 'I guess we can't have that, can we?'

Steve insisted on staying late to help.

'I'm the pilot,' he said. 'I have a vested interest in making my crewman winch proficient.'

'OK,' Tama nodded. 'I'll operate the winch and Steve can pretend to be the pilot.'

'Hey! I *am* the pilot.'

But Tama's attention was on Mikki. 'We'll run this as if it was for real. There'll be a standard winch patter between me and Steve, even though he'll be on the floor 'cos there's no room for him on the platform.'

Mikki climbed the metal rungs a little more slowly than Tama. Maybe she wasn't quite as confident as she'd made out to Andy.

Steve got into the spirit of the training exercise with enthusiasm.

'Target sighted,' he called. 'What's the target, Tama?'

'Train wreck,' Tama said. 'Carriages all squished into a narrow ravine. No chance of ground access.'

'Cool. Some nice dodgy flying through the mountains. Love it. Target sighted,' he repeated. 'Turning downwind.'

'Roger.' Tama was positioned by the winch machinery. 'I have the target. Checking winch power.'

Mikki was checking her harness. For the fourth time. She looked down from the platform. Ten metres onto concrete was still a long way off the floor. She looked up to find the encouragement she needed in Tama's quick glance. He thought she was ready and she was. She wanted this. She'd look pathetic if she backed out now that Tama had finally agreed to let her go to the next level.

'Clear to open door,' Steve called.

'Roger. Door back and locked. Bringing hook inboard. Hooking onto Mikki.'

The clunk of the carabiners fastening made Mikki's mouth dry out instantly but she didn't look down at the floor again. She checked that her pit pin was secure and then removed her seat belt. Then she kept her gaze on Tama.

'Moving Mikki to door.'

The patter was familiar because Mikki had learned and practised it already. Tama asked for permission to put Mikki onto the skids and she could feel the narrow, metal strip beneath her feet as she stood, still facing Tama in what would be the interior of the helicopter if this was for real.

Then all her weight was taken by the winch. Later in her training, she knew she would get equipment she might need, like the Thomas pack or a stretcher attached at this point to hang between her legs, but this time she only needed to think about herself.

She listened to the patter between Tama and Steve where permission was sought and gained to boom her out so that she hung just below the skids and then to winch her down to ground level. It was time to look down now and carefully estimate the distance.

'Minus eight,' Mikki called. 'Minus six…four, three, two…' And then her feet touched the floor of the hangar. Her hands shook just a little as she unhooked herself. She extended her right arm, with her hand palm upwards and gave a 'thumbs-up' signal to Tama to tell him to retract the hook.

He was smiling down at her. By the time they'd reversed the procedure and Mikki was safely back on the platform, he was grinning broadly.

Steve gave a cheer and he probably thought nothing of the fact that Tama gave Mikki a fierce hug. Just as well he didn't hear the words murmured in her ear.

'That's my girl,' Tama said. 'I'm proud of you, princess.'

Even better that Steve could have no idea of the effect of both Tama's touch and his pride in her. Mikki couldn't wait to do it again. To do more and to do it well enough to earn more of Tama's approval.

By the following week she could handle equipment as well as herself, and the ten-metre training had become routine. Nerves kicked in the day they had a false alarm call and got permission to use the air time to do Mikki's thirty-metre training from the helicopter, but again she passed the challenge with flying colours.

'We've only got your deployments in bush terrain to cover now,' Tama told her at the end of that week. 'Then you'll almost be ready for a real job.'

'Why not now?' Mikki asked. 'If it was a straightforward winch away from trees? I feel ready.'

'You're not ready,' Tama told her. 'Not yet. I'll tell you when.'

Apparently she was still not ready the following week and by then Mikki was really starting to feel frustrated. She could understand why she wasn't allowed to be winched around trees or boats or anything complicated but occasionally a job was straightforward. Like the car at the bottom of a steep gully or the tramper who'd broken his leg on a small, offshore island.

'I could do it,' Mikki pleaded.

'No,' Tama said. 'Not yet.'

'I've been in touch with MSF personnel,' Mikki told him. 'They're interviewing for a new intake in London in just over a month. I want to be there. *With* my qualification.'

But Tama wasn't about to bend. 'Make the most of being able to come on the missions with us as an observer. Watch and learn.'

She couldn't argue about simply watching the job

that came in later that morning. A badly injured crewman on a fishing vessel that was well out to sea. This job was dangerous and, of course, it would be Tama that would be winched down to the ship.

Mikki sat up front beside Steve.

'Bit different, this, isn't it?' he said once they were heading out to sea.

'Every job's different. It's part of what I love about doing this. You never know where you'll be going next or what you're going to find when you get there, but it's always exciting.'

Rather like her relationship with Tama. It was still working perfectly. Because they both knew it couldn't last? The completion of Mikki's training was almost in sight. Or it would be as soon as Tama allowed her to do some genuine winch work. She already had the paperwork ready to make her application to MSF. An application she intended to hand in at the interview in London. All it needed was the addition of her certification that she was qualified for helicopter work.

It was the perfect recipe for making the most of what they had and Mikki, at least, was still blown away by the most intense physical relationship she had ever experienced. The sex was like what she'd just said to Steve about helicopter work. She never knew quite what to expect in the way of location or content, but it was always, *always* exciting.

Like the day when their hunger for each other had built during their hours of working together to such a degree the passion had taken over the moment the door of Tama's flat had slammed behind them. They hadn't even got any further than the narrow hallway.

Mikki could still feel the power of that encounter now—weeks later. She could feel the wall behind her back and Tama's hands on her body. His strength as he cupped her bottom and carried her weight as she clung, with her hands around his neck and her legs around his waist. The relentless journey he took them both on until they reached an unforgettable climax.

Mikki stole a glance at Steve but he was busy checking GPS co-ordinates and looking out for a sighting of their target. As she should also be doing. Tama was in the back with Alistair. Out of sight.

But not yet out of mind.

As an antidote for the desire she had conjured up, Mikki deliberately tried to banish the memory of the wildest sex she'd ever had by remembering something as different as possible. An ordinary bed. Slow, careful sex where every touch was a caress.

No. That wasn't helping. Desire still curled strongly within her.

What about the night they'd both been too tired to do anything but fall asleep together, Tama having one arm beneath her head and the other draped carelessly over her midriff.

No. In its own way, just as memorable. She had fallen asleep feeling so…safe.

She would miss Tama when she left, that was for sure, but it was something she was going to have to deal with. Knowing all along that that point was coming would surely make it easier. Less stressful, anyway.

'Target sighted,' came from one of the men in the back of the helicopter. 'Nine o'clock.'

'Roger.' The helicopter banked as Steve changed direction. 'Target in sight,' he said a moment later. He changed channels on the radio to put him in contact with Control. 'Patch me through to the skipper,' he ordered.

Mikki was impressed with the way Steve kept two lines of communication open then, one with the skipper of the fishing vessel and the other with his crew. He instructed the skipper to turn downwind and keep his speed up enough to be able to control his steering in the ocean swell.

'Turning base leg,' he told Alistair. 'Clear to open door.'

'Roger. Door back and locked. Deploying Hi Line.'

'Roger. Skipper?' Steve raised his voice and spoke slowly and clearly. 'The line is on its way down. Catch it, but do not attach it to any part of your vessel. I repeat. Do *not* attach the line to anything.'

'Roger.' The skipper's voice had a marked foreign accent. 'I hear you loud and clear.'

The Hi Line was an extra connection, held by people on the boat and attached to Tama's harness at the other end. He would be winched down far enough away from the danger of becoming entangled in the mast or aerials of the vessel and then he would be pulled in sideways by the Hi Line being retracted.

'Moving Tama to door,' Alistair said. 'Clear skids.'

'Clear skids.'

Mikki turned so that she could watch. She saw Tama hanging below the skids and then beginning his descent. She looked further down and could see the bristling spikes of the mast and aerials on the boat, along with containers and fishing tackle and all sorts of other obstructions. She could also see the pitch and roll of the vessel as it negotiated a fairly heavy sea.

Tama's voice was calm as he counted off his descent. 'Minus fifteen… Minus ten… Minus five…'

Maybe it was that calmness that was Mikki's undoing. Did he not see how dangerous this was? What if the lines got caught on a projection of some kind? Or the fishing crew hadn't understood directions and had wound the Hi Line around some solid object? What if the boat suddenly rolled or changed its pitch just as he was touching down on the deck? He could break his legs or his back.

He could be *killed*.

And Mikki would never see that quirky, one-sided smile again. Or the twinkle of mischief in those dark eyes. She would never taste the sweetness of his kisses or feel the touch of his hands on her body. She would never feel the swell of her heart that came from the particular pride of doing something that impressed him.

Fear blindsided her like a blast of icy air and Mikki felt chilled to the bone.

So unexpected. And disturbing. It should have been banished by seeing Tama arrive safely on the deck where he unhooked himself and his gear and then moved to crouch beside the injured man, but it still lurked. Unwelcome and unsettling.

Was it going to be like this when she left on the next stage of her career and wouldn't be seeing Tama again?

Was this what it was like to be in love with someone? To care about them so much that the thought of losing them was terrifying?

No.

She wasn't in love with Tama. However good this not-quite-real relationship was, she knew with absolute certainty that it was a one-off experience in her life. All the more thrilling because of the hero-worship aspect she'd been carrying from the first moment she'd met him. A bit embarrassing now to remember that she'd had that photograph of him folded up in the back pocket of her jeans.

Besides, when she left she'd know he was still alive. It would be her choice to leave his company, not something that was being ripped from her by fate. They could stay in touch by email perhaps. Even see each other again one day. Maybe part of that fear in watching Tama's descent had been because she knew she might be doing it herself before very long. She had taken apprehension for her own safety, blown it out of proportion and transferred it to Tama.

The patient had his crushed hand and badly broken arm dressed and splinted and pain relief administered, and then he was made secure in the nappy harness and preparations were made to bring him up to the aircraft.

No, Mikki repeated silently with more confidence. Tama was an amazing man but totally the wrong person for any woman to fall in love with. It would be more than stupid to fall for someone who'd made it very clear he would never return such emotions.

Mikki had grown out of being stupid a very long time ago.

Something wasn't right.

Maybe he was just tired. Nerve endings frayed after that big job this afternoon. Exciting but dangerous stuff, winching onto boats on the open sea. There was often a downside to that kind of adrenaline rush.

That could explain why Tama was sitting here, his

lunch only half-eaten and his coffee getting cold, feeling like he was missing something.

Something important.

Looking up, he could see Mikki sitting at the other end of the table with a pile of paperwork in front of her. He knew she was studying for the written paper she would need to sit soon. Not that she needed to. Tama could bet his pupil was going to get a hundred per cent of the answers correct. She would really put the pressure on to finish her practical training then, wouldn't she?

Did she have any idea how dangerous it could be? He had been thinking about it on his way down to the ship that morning. Feeling grateful that it was him doing this and that he didn't have to worry about Mikki getting something wrong. Getting herself tangled in obstacles or timing her landing on a pitching deck incorrectly. Smashing herself on an unforgiving metal surface.

Was that why he was dragging his feet about letting her go to the next stage of her winching training? Would he feel the same way about it if she wasn't sharing his bed as well as his work environment?

An unsettling thought that made him a little more uneasy.

It was no surprise that Mikki sensed the observation she was under and flicked her gaze up from the printed papers in front of her. For a moment they simply held the eye contact—a silent and intimate communication they'd become expert in over the last… Good grief—it was nearly a month since that astonishing night up on the mountain. Getting close to a record as far as Tama's involvement with women went.

No wonder he was nervous!

Mikki smiled at him. The kind of smile he had come to watch for. He loved seeing that she was happy. Happy to be where she was and doing what she was doing. Happy to be close to *him*. Tama smiled back but inside that feeling that something wasn't right grew bigger. It sat like a heavy weight in his gut.

'You're staring at me,' Mikki said.

'Am I?' Tama shrugged.

'Yeah.' Mikki's smile widened. 'Ask me a question.'

'What about?'

'What do you think?' Mikki rolled her eyes and then tapped the papers on the table.

Of course. What a stupid question. Mikki was focussed on only one thing in her life. Getting her damn qualification so she could disappear off to the other side of the world and get on with all the dangerous adventures she was so keen to experience. It had been her focus from the moment she'd set foot on station, hadn't it? Did she see him as anything more than what he'd jokingly suggested as being an extra part of the curriculum?

Tama suppressed a sigh. 'Fine. What's the maximum working load for winching?'

'Six hundred pounds.'

'Average cable speed?'

'At six hundred pounds, one hundred feet per minute.'

'What's the emergency guillotine?'

'An electrically fired device the pilot can activate that will cut the cable.'

Tama was asking questions automatically. He didn't have to think hard which made it too easy to have part of his brain still chewing over the cause of that uneasy sensation. Obviously it had something to do with Mikki.

Maybe he was feeling…used. Faced with the focus she was displaying right now, he had to wonder if she had seen a closer relationship with him as a means of speeding up the process of getting what she wanted.

If the thought had occurred to him a month ago, he wouldn't have been bothered. This was a temporary arrangement that most men would think was a dream. A gorgeous, *amazing* woman who was willing to be in his bed as often as he wished with no strings attached. No demands. No expectations that he could and should be offering more than he was prepared to offer.

Why the hell should motivation be a problem? Why did he feel like he was being used?

'What's the thumbwheel?'

'A wheel located on the shrouded upper portion of the hand grip. It controls direction and speed. Moves upwards to lift a load and downwards to lower it.'

Mikki's eyes were shining. She knew she was getting the answers correct. She knew she was well on the way to getting exactly what she wanted.

Like she always had?

The resentment with which Tama had viewed his new recruit surfaced for the first time in weeks. She was a princess, he reminded himself. Spoilt. Yes, she may be capable and courageous and able to do this job as well as him but she hadn't had to fight to get here, had she? There must have been a string of people in her life making things easier for her. Housekeepers and gardeners and probably chauffeurs. He was just the latest, wasn't he?

A kind of employee who was being paid a bonus. She'd move on with her life and he'd be forgotten.

The heavy feeling developed sharp edges.

'I'm good, huh?' Mikki was smiling again. 'Do you think I'll pass the written paper?'

'Yeah. I guess.'

'You don't sound very pleased about it.'

Tama shoved his chair back and stood up, needing movement. He picked up his unfinished sandwich and went to drop it in the bin. 'Maybe I'm not.'

'Why?' Mikki's smile had vanished.

'You're already pushing to do more than you're ready to do. I don't want you to have any more ammunition.'

'Oh…' The tone was thoughtful. 'You're determined to put the brakes on, aren't you, Tama?'

'No. I'm determined that you remain safe and become proficient when you're ready.'

'I've only got a month left. I'm going to be at that interview in London, Tama. With or without my qualification. I would just *prefer* to have it.'

'So you can go off and kill yourself in some war zone? What is with you, Mikki? Why are you so hell bent on doing such a bloody dangerous job?'

'Look who's talking! You spent this morning doing what looked like an exceptionally dangerous job.'

'That's different.'

'Why? Why was it any less dangerous because you were doing it?'

'It wasn't. I have the experience to deal with it.'

'So teach me! That's what I'm here for. If you want me to be safe, then do your job and teach me how to be.'

Tama stared at her. Do his job? She did see him as an employee, didn't she? Just a step up from a gardener or something.

'I was actually worried about you during that winch,'

Mikki continued heatedly. 'I wouldn't have tried to stop you doing it, though. I respect your right to do what you want with your life.'

She was worried about him? The hard knot in Tama's gut changed shape and felt odd. He couldn't identify how it made him feel.

'You're as bad as my father,' Mikki snapped. 'Trying to control me and what I want to do with my life in the name of safety.'

OK. Much easier to stay angry than try and analyse that peculiar sensation, and the mention of Mikki's father made it a no-brainer. The anger grew.

'I'm nothing like your father,' he snapped back. 'I wouldn't have let you do this in the first place. I certainly wouldn't have tried to make it easy for you.'

Mikki's jaw dropped. 'What the hell is that supposed to mean?'

'You know as well as I do.'

'*What?*' The grim, imperious tone was enough to push Tama that bit further. To dredge up and let go of the resentment that had been there right from the start. Buried but not entirely forgotten.

'That your father set this training up. That if the whole helicopter rescue service wasn't dependent on the money he generates for us, there's no way you would have been taken on like this. You would have had to wait for the next intake, like everybody else. You wouldn't have got anywhere near this station until next year at the earliest and you would have been competing with a lot of very fit, very keen guys. No guarantee you would have made the cut.'

Not entirely true. Tama pushed back the memory of

just how competent Mikki had shown herself to be at that pre-requisite challenge. For some obscure reason he didn't have time to figure out he was very, very angry and he was going to win this argument.

Maybe he already had. Mikki was as pale as he'd ever seen her.

'That's not true,' she whispered. 'It *can't* be true.'

'You think I'm lying?' She didn't trust him, did she? Didn't trust his professional judgement and didn't even trust him to tell the truth. 'Why don't you ask him yourself?'

'I will.' Mikki's chin came up and the rest of her body followed. She was pulling her mobile phone from the pocket of her overalls as she turned and walked outside without a backward glance.

Tama could see her outside a few moments later. Pacing back and forth as she held the phone to her ear.

Had she really not known?

Why had he told her?

His anger evaporated and that nasty, uneasy feeling was there again. With teeth now. Gnawing at his gut.

What the hell had he just done?

CHAPTER TEN

MIKKI couldn't get hold of her father.

He had probably turned his mobile phone off because he was on a plane or in the middle of some important meeting that would end up increasing his net worth by another million or so. The kind of money that made it possible to be a major source of funding for a rescue helicopter service.

She didn't need to speak to him, anyway. She didn't *want* to speak to him.

Holding her phone to her ear and pacing about was simply a means of getting a few minutes to herself. To try and sort through the chaotic jumble of her thoughts.

She knew perfectly well Tama was right. It was just the kind of thing her father would do, and he had the power to do it. Mikki kept pacing, her humiliation growing with every extra shred of back-up evidence her mind was only too happy to produce.

Like how miraculous it had been to get that acceptance to try out for a place on the crew.

And how much Tama hadn't wanted her there. She had been so aware of his disdain that first day she'd turned up on his station, and look at the way he'd just walked off when she'd passed that physical challenge. It had been Andy who'd congratulated her and welcomed her on board. The station manager. The middle man between the crew and the board of directors that involved her father.

The way he'd called her 'princess'! Josh must have known, too. Hadn't Tama jumped on him only recently when he'd made a crack about her being given the 'royal treatment'?

The conversation with her father when she'd known there was something odd in the way he'd said Tama's name. He'd lied to her, hadn't he, when he'd said he didn't know her instructor?

Anger edged into the humiliation that came from the horrible notion that Tama and Josh had only agreed to take her on because they'd been told to comply with the request of someone who had major strings they could tweak.

No wonder Tama had glossed over that first job when her performance had been less than impressive. Had he been lying all along, too? Spoon-feeding her so that she could pass and get her coveted qualification because her father had requested the prize on her behalf?

This was all a sham.

Including Tama's attraction to her? He'd said it more than once, hadn't he? That she was 'special'. He hadn't meant *her*, though, had he? She'd been special because of who her father was. Had he seen sleeping with her as part of a game? A bit of fun that didn't really matter because she didn't have to go by the same rules as everybody else?

The anger grew. Mikki was angry enough to march

back inside. Into the messroom where Tama was—astonishingly—cleaning up the bench.

'I'm leaving,' Mikki announced. 'I'll find another helicopter service that'll take me on for training. One that has no connection whatsoever to my father. One where I'll actually get treated professionally. Judged on what I'm capable of doing and not who I am. Or, worse, who my father happens to be.'

Tama didn't interrupt the tirade. He paused in his task, the tea-towel dangling from his hand, his head inclined enough to show he was listening. And he waited until it was clear Mikki had had her say.

'I guess you *didn't* know about it,' he said evenly.

'You thought I did?' Mikki shook her head in disbelief. 'You thought I'd just go ahead and take advantage of a privilege I hadn't earned?' Her outward breath was an incredulous huff. 'Of course! You thought I was a receptionist or something, didn't you? An airhead. You actually believed me when I said I had a manicure booked.'

Tama was twisting the tea-towel in his hands. 'That was a long time ago. I didn't know you then.'

'You don't know me now,' Mikki spat.

That *hurt*, dammit!

She'd spent so much time with this man. Admired him so much. Given him every ounce of her strength and abilities in trying to prove herself and win his approval.

And that was only part of it now. She'd given him everything she had to give in bed as well, and that made her want to cringe in shame.

It counted for nothing. All of it. Tama thought she was simply a spoilt…princess. That she got what she wanted in life handed to her. That it was all just a game. He didn't know her and he never would because she was getting out of here. Escaping. Leaving this station.

Leaving Tama.

Anger, shame, humiliation and something even darker that felt like…grief jostled each other and Mikki had the horrible sensation it was all too much and she was about to burst into tears.

She opened her mouth with the intention of delivering some cutting remark to try and salvage just a scrap of pride before turning on her heel and walking away. But no words came out.

And Tama had the nerve to be standing there looking angry himself.

'I know you better than you think,' he said. 'Yes, I admit I didn't like the idea of you coming here by cutting through the red tape. And you turned up and you looked exactly how I expected you to look. Tiny and pretty and…and fragile. I was all set to give you a challenge I didn't think you'd be able to pass so I wouldn't have to train you.'

Mikki had opened her mouth again to interrupt. He had thought she was pretty? Was it a compliment or an insult? She closed her mouth.

'And you know what?' Tama continued without a pause. 'You surprised me. Turned out you were determined. Clever. Brave. You blew me away the day of the HUET training, you know that? I actually started to feel proud to have you on my crew that day. And since then?'

He had raised his eyebrows. He was saying nice things about her. Amazing things. He thought she was clever? Brave? It almost sounded like he really admired her so why was he still looking so angry? He was starting to sound angry as well and Mikki had to throw confusion into the mix of her reaction. What was he going to say now?

Something about that survival training and their time on the mountain?

About their relationship?

Was he going to tell her he would miss her when she was gone?

That he didn't want her to leave?

Mikki's breath caught in her throat and stayed there.

'Since then...no, even before then, I'd decided you weren't really a princess. That you were prepared to work bloody hard and even fight for what you wanted if you had to. And now you're going to walk out? Without the qualification you want so badly?'

The tea-towel was now a scrunched-up ball in his hands. One that was flung sideways into the sink, giving the impression that Tama was disgusted.

'You're right,' he said bitterly. 'I *don't* know you.'

This was the time to say he never would. Too bad. That she didn't care what he thought of her. But that wasn't true, was it? She cared a lot about what Tama thought of her. That was why it hurt so much to think this training had been a set-up. She winced as the tea-towel landed in the sink with a dull thud because she could suddenly see this from Tama's point of view.

She'd been behaving like a princess, hadn't she? Nagging to get what she wanted. Not prepared to trust his judgement on whether or not she was ready. And when he'd said no again, what had she done?

Stamped her foot and thrown a tantrum. She was halfway through throwing her toys—and her qualification—out of the cot.

No wonder he looked disgusted.

Mikki really wanted to cry now. She had never felt so stupid. Small and useless and…still angry, but the anger was being directed inwards now.

She couldn't think of anything to say. A silent plea for something—she had no idea what—formed in the silence that fell.

The plea was answered in a very unexpected way.

Their pagers sounded.

Tama read the message. He went to the phone and spoke briefly.

'We've got a job,' he said to Mikki. 'Are you coming?'

Mikki swallowed. 'For winching?'

Tama eyed her steadily. Oh, God, did he think she was still nagging? Trying to throw her father's weight around?

'Don't know yet,' he said. She couldn't read his expression. His face was set in grim lines and his eyes were so dark they looked black. 'If it is,' he continued calmly, 'it's yours. You can have the job, Mikki. And if you do it as well as you've done every other challenge, I'll sign you off as proficient. And then you can leave if that's what you want.'

And it was Tama who walked out. Heading towards the office to look at the maps and get ready for the new mission.

Mikki dragged in a breath. And then another. This felt like a turning point for something. Her career? Her relationship with Tama? Her *life*?

It didn't feel like there was a choice involved, however. Her feet seemed to move by themselves. Taking her towards the office.

Taking on the job.

Was this it?

The last mission he'd ever go on with Mikki?

From the information they'd received it sounded like it would be a winch job. A teenager had been seen climbing a beachside cliff and he now appeared to be stuck about halfway up. He could be seen hunched on a narrow ledge but wasn't responding to any attempts at communication.

Emergency services were at the top but the area was dangerous. Notorious for being unstable. Too risky for anyone to abseil down because it was too likely to send a rockfall onto the ledge, and it would be impossible to climb up with any gear. Nobody could figure out how the boy had managed to climb up in the first place. Or why.

It didn't matter why.

Tama turned his head from where he sat in the winch operator's seat. Mikki was sitting on the other side and she was staring resolutely from the window on her left. All Tama could see was the back of her helmet.

No. It didn't matter why the boy had chosen to climb a dangerous cliff face. It didn't matter why or how Mikki had won her chance to try out for the team either. She was only here because she had proved worthy of the opportunity and he shouldn't have suggested otherwise.

Why had he? Why had he held onto some immature jealousy that Mikki had grown up with all the advantages money could buy? With the idea that everything had been easy for her and she couldn't imagine what it was like to inhabit his planet? That she would look down on him if she really knew what his upbringing had been like.

That didn't seem to matter anymore either. In so many ways, he and Mikki were the same. He'd said that to her, when? When he'd been hell bent on getting her into his bed? It didn't mean it wasn't true.

They wanted the same things in life. The adrenaline rush of this job. The satisfaction of knowing you'd saved a life. The thrill of sex without a commitment that might have unpleasant long-term consequences, such as interfering with a career you were passionate about.

Except that one day Mikki was going to change her mind about that, wasn't she? When she met the right person.

Why wasn't *he* the right person?

Did he want to be?

No.

Yes.

Dammit! Tama could feel the lines of his scowl etching deeper into his forehead. He felt confused and he hated feeling confused. Maybe what he really wanted was to have the choice.

Maybe he didn't want Mikki walking out of his life as though it meant nothing to her. As though *he* meant nothing to her.

'Target sighted.' But Steve sounded preoccupied. 'I'm getting a call from Control here. I'll patch you guys through.'

'The boy's name is Tim,' Tama heard the voice of someone at the control centre. 'The police are taking his mother to the scene. She's received a text message that makes this look like it's a suicide attempt.'

Tama groaned. This changed everything.

'Copy that,' Mikki said briskly. 'Do you know his age?'

'Fifteen.'

'Any background?'

'Sister died last year. Brain tumour. Single mother. She says he's been very withdrawn since then. In trouble at school.'

'Drugs?' Tama queried succinctly.

'Unknown. Mother doesn't think so.'

Steve was circling above the scene. 'How close should I go?' he asked. 'I don't want to push him into doing anything stupid.'

Mikki was staring intently from her window. 'He's just sitting,' she said. 'He's got his head on his knees. I don't think he's going to jump in a hurry.'

'You still there, Control?' Tama asked. 'Is the boy answering his phone?'

'No. It's going straight to voicemail. Either turned off or dead.'

'And he can't hear anyone from the top?'

'Negative. No response, anyway.'

'The ledge is quite long.' Mikki was still peering downwards. 'If I land well away, it won't be too threatening but I'll be able to talk to him.'

'No.' Tama changed channels so that only Mikki and Steve could hear him. 'The cliff's unstable and, as far as we know, this lad doesn't want to be rescued. This isn't a straightforward job, Mikki. We'll land on top and change places. Alistair can operate the winch and I'll go down.'

'No.' Mikki's head turned. Her face was still as grim as it had been ever since their confrontation in the mess-room but her voice was calm. More determined than

Tama had ever heard it. 'I can do this. I want to do this. You said this was my job, Tama.'

He had. And he'd told her in the past that he kept his word. That she could trust him. This might be his last opportunity to give her anything and he owed her this chance, didn't he? His hesitation was only brief.

'Fine,' he growled. 'But you don't get close enough to touch him.' He wasn't having this kid grab her and then send them both plummeting to their deaths on the rocks below.

Mikki said nothing. She was checking her harness.

'If he moves…' Tama said a minute or two later when the side door was open and locked. 'If he even *looks* like moving, I'm pulling you out. Got it?'

'Roger.' Mikki was looking past him. Waiting for the hook to be brought inboard.

It seemed only a very short time after that to Tama being in control of lowering Mikki. Carefully. Fortunately, it wasn't at all windy, which made it relatively safe to put her down so close to a cliff.

Relatively.

She looked tiny on the end of the cable and the responsibility was weighing heavily on Tama.

This was why he had been trying to slow her training schedule down. He'd known, at some level, how it would feel to be there when Mikki was putting herself in danger. Close enough to watch but not necessarily close enough to protect her.

And he wanted to protect this woman.

When he next met Trevor Elliot he might have to shake the man's hand for succeeding in keeping Mikki safe thus far in her life.

Why *did* she want to do this?

'Minus six…' Mikki's voice sounded as clear as a bell inside his helmet. 'Four…two…'

Tama could see her feet touch the ledge and he tried to help Steve keep the helicopter as still as possible in its hover by sheer willpower.

Mikki tested her footing and the stability of the ledge. She unhooked herself and held the cable out, signalling for Tama to retract it. The boy hadn't moved. He still sat, a miserable hunched figure, about ten metres from Mikki.

She didn't move any closer and Tama let out a breath he hadn't realised he was holding.

He nodded his approval a second later as Mikki crouched down, both to make herself seem less threatening and to give her a more stable position on the ledge.

'Hey, Tim,' he heard her call softly. 'I'm Mikki.'

There was no response.

Steve took the chopper higher on the way to touching down in the clear area at the top of the cliff but Mikki obviously hadn't thought to push her microphone out of the way and Tama could hear her with perfect clarity even though her figure was unrecognisable from this distance. He adjusted his own microphone, so he could speak without Mikki hearing him unless he wanted her to, but he could still hear her.

Her voice would never be unrecognisable. If he never heard it again after today, he would always remember it. So clear. Often eager, almost always resolute. So soft sometimes, it kind of reverberated in his bones.

'Are you hurt?' Mikki was asking now. 'Is it OK if I come a bit closer?'

No! Tama's lips formed the words silently. Don't do that. But he could hear other noises that suggested

Mikki was moving. Squeaks and a soft thud and a tiny catch of breath, as though the footing wasn't as steady as she had expected.

'Let's get down,' he said to Steve. 'I want to get somewhere where I can see what's going on. See if there's a way of at least getting a rope down to her.'

Mikki's voice continued in his helmet as the chopper landed and Tama moved swiftly to liaise with the emergency services already on the scene.

A distraught-looking woman who had to be Tim's mother was being helped from a police car. Fire service personnel, ambulance officers and police were gathered at a point that allowed them to see what was happening, judging by the grim intensity of the group.

'*Please!*' he heard the woman beg. 'Try his phone again. I *have* to talk to him. He's…he's all I have now…'

Mikki's voice continued as a kind of background. Quiet and calm. Trying to win the boy's confidence and trust or at least get him to listen and buy some time.

Had she had any kind of training in counselling or negotiation? Tama hadn't thought to ask. She seemed to be doing all right, though. She was probably as good at this as she was at everything else she was determined to master.

By the time Tama reached the point where he could see down the cliff, Mikki was getting a response.

Everybody was staring at the two figures, now hunched much closer together on the ledge, but only Tama could hear what was going on.

'How do *you* know?' The teenager sounded angry. 'You don't know *anything*.'

'I was fifteen once,' Mikki said. 'And my life wasn't so great either.'

'Your sister didn't die.'

'No. I'm really sorry about that, Tim. It was a horrible thing to happen.'

Her mother had died, Tama thought. She did know how bad things could be.

'Mum hates me. She thinks it was my fault.'

'That's not true, Tim.'

'She wishes it had been me instead, then.'

'What makes you say that?'

'She stopped talking to me. She stopped even looking at me.' The words sounded as if they were being dragged out but he wanted to talk. That was a good sign. Tama silently encouraged the boy. 'It was like…I don't exist anymore. Even when I got into big trouble at school and she *had* to notice me, she didn't care. She didn't even care enough to tell me off.'

The sound of the sobs that came then was heart-breaking. Choked and despairing. Quiet enough for Tama to still hear what Mikki was saying.

'When people are really hurt, Tim, like when they lose someone they love very much, they can get scared. Too scared to let themselves love other people. They can pretend they don't care because that's the only way they think they can protect themselves from getting hurt all over again.'

Tama closed his eyes. Was she talking about herself here? She could almost be talking about *him*. Had he ever let himself love anyone after his mother had gone? Trusted that anyone would want to stay around long enough to make it safe?

'And when *you* love someone and you lose them, it hurts, Tim. It hurt when you lost your sister and now you feel like you've lost your mum, even though she's still around. Yes?'

'Yeah…'

'And when something hurts so much you can't bear it, you want to die because you think it's the only way to make the pain go away.'

Tama heard a sound like a groan. The sound of someone in pain.

'It *is* the only way.'

'*No.*' Mikki's voice had a quiet passion in it. A sincerity that was compelling. 'Feeling like this, Tim— feeling so bad you want to die—it's like being in the worst storm you can imagine. With hail and sleet and thunder and lightning, and every bolt of lightning feels like it's going through your body and you just want to curl up because of the pain.' He could hear Mikki draw in a slow breath. 'What happens after a storm, Tim?'

She waited for the response. When it finally came, it was sullen. 'Dunno.'

'Yes, you do.' Mikki waited again. 'Eventually, what happens?'

Only silence greeted the question.

'Does the thunder and lightning stop?'

'I s'pose.'

'Does the hail and rain stop?'

'Yeah.'

'And then what happens? What happens when the storm ends or gets blown away and the sky is clear? What comes out?'

This time Mikki didn't let the silence continue. 'The sun, Tim. Maybe it's patchy and weak to start with, but it always comes back and one day you know it's going to be blazing. You're going to want to be outside and maybe go to the beach and be warm and feel safe that there's no storm in sight. Maybe you'll never be in a storm quite that bad again.'

Mikki sounded slightly out of breath now. The little catch in her voice as she took in enough air to keep going touched Tama in a very deep place. She really believed what she was saying. She really wanted this lonely, miserable child to believe her.

'That's what life is like, Tim. Being happy is the sunny time. Nobody's happy *all* the time but it's because life's like that that we know how good it is to feel happy. And…and if you die in a storm then you'll never feel the sun again and it's worth hanging on, it really is, because you'll get through this.'

'No, I won't.'

'Yes, you will. You don't have to do it by yourself. If it was a storm you could find shelter. With life you can get shelter, too.'

'How?'

'Through people. People that care. Especially people that love you.'

'Nobody loves me.'

'Why is your mum coming here, then?'

'My mum's coming? Is she here?'

'I expect she's arrived by now. And she's scared, Tim. She doesn't want to lose you.'

'But I threw my phone away. How did she know where I am?'

'People saw you climbing the cliff.'

'Where are they?'

'Up the top. Hey, don't move, Tim! Oh… God!'

Tama saw Mikki reach out and grab Tim's arm. He saw the boy's foot slip and a cascade of small rocks went over the edge of the ledge. He heard the horrified gasp from the onlookers and a similar sound from both Mikki and Tim seemed magnified in his earphones.

'Help!' Tim cried. 'I don't want to fall.'

It was enough. Too much. Tama turned and ran back to the idling helicopter. He grabbed a harness and gave terse instructions to Steve and Alistair.

'Mikki's got a nappy harness she can put on Tim. If he's co-operative, the safest way to do this is going to be if I go down and bring them both up, one at a time. That ledge is crumbling.'

The minute that ticked past seemed much longer. So did the next. And then they were airborne and Tama was talking to Mikki.

'Try to move as little as possible but get the nappy harness onto Tim. Find an anchor you can hang onto. Try one of those shrubby trees or a larger rock. I'm coming down.'

Another minute and he was outside the helicopter. And then he was descending smoothly. Counting off the distance. Keeping his voice calm, even though he saw another boulder come free from the ledge and bounce down the cliff to smash into the rocks at the shoreline.

Mikki was standing, her back to the cliff and her feet planted on an area that looked stable enough. She had her arms around the boy and she had managed to get the harness on him.

'It's OK, Tim,' he heard her saying. 'Tama's the best there is. You're safe. He's going to hook your harness onto his and take you up to the helicopter.'

'*No-o*! I'm scared.'

'I know, honey, but it's safe, I promise. Everything's going to be fine.'

Tama found a smile to reassure Tim as his feet touched the ledge. 'Put your arms around my neck. Hang on, buddy.'

It was hard to turn his head in the panicked grip but Tama had to look back at Mikki. He almost wished he hadn't.

He'd never seen her look this afraid and it went through him like physical pain.

'I'll be right back to get you,' he said gruffly. 'Don't move.'

He couldn't look down again until he was standing on the skids and Alistair was helping pull Tim to safety within the helicopter.

Then he was ready to go down again and rescue Mikki. He looked down past his feet where he could see Mikki still hanging onto the trunk of the small, dead-looking tree.

And then he saw the tree move and her feet slip as the ledge beneath them crumbled.

He heard her soft, stricken cry.

She was hanging. The only thing preventing her from falling to the rocks below was the grip she had on a skinny tree trunk that was clearly as unstable as everything else on this damned cliff.

Tama was about to lose her.

For ever.

'Get me down,' he barked at Alistair. '*Now!*'

CHAPTER ELEVEN

MIKKI was about to die.

There was nothing below her feet.

Just space. A huge space that she knew ended where the waves were crashing onto those unforgiving rocks. She'd heard the rumble and crack of dislodged boulders—a sound that went on and on to let her know just how far she was about to fall.

This wasn't supposed to happen. OK, she'd been happy to flirt with death. She'd pushed hard for the opportunity to do exactly that, but she had never really believed she wouldn't survive. That she would gamble and lose.

She could hear the harsh sound of her own breathing inside her helmet. From outside, now that the rockfall had finally ceased, she could hear a kind of roaring. Faint shouting? Mechanical noises? The roaring of her own thoughts was louder.

Images, like movie trailers. Of the future she had so carefully planned to be full of adventure and new experiences. Enough danger to make her appreciate being alive. Thrills and spills with the cushion of knowing that one day she would have had enough and she'd find a wonderful partner and the safe haven of a family of her own.

Children of her own that she could love with all her heart. Just the way her mother had loved her right to her last moments.

Her breath rushed out in a strange combination of grief and wry mirth. Wasn't it the past that was supposed to flash past in the final moments of your life, not the future?

Her hands were going numb. Her grip so tight the blood supply was probably cut off but she couldn't loosen her hold on that pathetic half-dead tree trunk. Not without just giving up, and she'd never been one to give up. She couldn't hold on much longer, though. When all feeling had gone, she'd lose the ability to control her muscles and that would be that.

Mikki squeezed her eyes shut and could feel a tear escape. Sorry, Dad, she thought. You were right.

Sorry, Tama, she thought next. You were right, too. I wasn't ready for this.

I'm not ready to die.

Panic was edging closer. Fear threatened to obliterate any rational thought.

'Help…' Were the words coming from her lips or still part of the roaring inside her head? 'I need…*help*.'

Her hands were starting to slip. Mikki kicked her feet in a futile attempt to find a foothold. A scream was building inside her head. Gaining strength. She just needed enough breath to release it.

The voice inside her helmet came loud and clear then.

Soft and compelling.

'Be still,' it said.

And somehow it created a barrier to hold back the

scream. Mikki knew that voice. She trusted it. It went with such a solid presence. With arms that could hold her and make her feel safe. It was all Mikki could wish for right then. All she could ever wish for.

The arms were here now, too. Strong and sure. Mikki felt some kind of strap being fastened around her body but when it came time for her to let go of her handhold she couldn't do it.

'Let go, Mikki,' Tama said. 'You're safe now. I've got you.'

Things blurred then. Her awareness of being winched up to the helicopter was hazy. She was strapped into her seat. Tim was there, too, but not for long. It seemed only seconds until they landed on the cliff top and then Tim had his mother's arms around him and they were both crying. Being led away and cared for by other people.

Mikki couldn't cry. She felt totally numb. She barely heard the words of congratulations and relief from Steve and Alistair. Tama deserved the praise, not her. He had saved the day. She had failed spectacularly. Would Tama say anything? Not on the trip back to station, apparently. It was silent.

Their shift was over by the time they got back. Steve was busy with the helicopter. Alistair went home. Tama had gone to do something in the office. Eventually, Mikki sat with a drink that had been hot when someone had made it for her but it was stone cold now. The shock was beginning to recede but it was still hard to think straight.

Tama returned. He stood not far away but Mikki had her forehead resting on the palm of her hand and she didn't want to look up and see her failure reflected back at her. She waited for deserved words of recrimination.

'You OK?'

'Yes.' It hadn't been what she'd expected. The enquiry regarding her welfare was almost enough to make her cry. He sounded like he genuinely cared. 'No,' she added. 'Oh, I don't know.' With a resigned sigh Mikki raised her gaze. 'You saved my life, Tama. Thank you.'

He grunted as he pulled out a chair and sat down. It was a noncommittal sound.

'I rang the hospital. Tim's going to be fine, I think. Both he and his mother have agreed to get help. She's going to have treatment for her depression and they both need counselling to get through this period. The psychologist sounded optimistic.' Tama cleared his throat. 'There was a message Tim's mother wanted passed on to you. She said to say thank you. Very much.'

Mikki gave her head a tiny shake. 'I didn't do much. He just needed someone to talk to.'

'No. He needed someone to talk to who understood.' Tama was silent for a moment. 'I need to apologise,' he said then.

Mikki's chin came up sharply. 'What on earth for?'

'For ever thinking you were a princess. That you'd have no idea what real life was like. You've been through it yourself, haven't you?'

'Through what?'

'The kind of hell that kid was in. Thinking the only way out was to kill himself.'

'I guess.' Mikki closed her eyes as she took a deep breath. 'I never got to the point of thinking about suicide but things were rough for a few years after Mum died.'

'Your father was too scared to love you.'

'And I tried to get him to notice by getting myself into trouble. I was worse than Tim. I got into alcohol and car racing. I discovered the thrill of cheating death. And when I pushed it far enough I got an even better prize. My dad noticed me. He woke up and started living again and…it was all the more exciting doing dangerous things because I knew it made him worried. Made him show that he cared about me. I hope Tim hasn't started a life of chasing danger.'

'I think he got enough of a fright today to cure him of wanting to try it again.'

Mikki's chuckle was wry. 'I think I might have, too.'

'Oh?'

'I hope I never get that close to killing myself again.'

'So do I.' The words were a growl.

'I won't be trying, that's for sure. It was…different this time.'

'How?' Tama was watching her closely.

'I was scared,' Mikki admitted. 'Really scared.'

'You've done scary things before. That underwater escape training was hardly a picnic.'

Mikki nodded. 'That's true. And that was like all the other times I've been that scared. I survived and then I got that amazing realisation that I was safe and it made me feel like…nothing else can.'

Tama was nodding, too. He knew that feeling. Of course he did. That had been the first moment of connection between them, hadn't it? That they'd both felt the same.

'But this time it's different. It hasn't happened. I still feel…scared.'

Tama frowned. He reached out and took hold of her

hand. 'You don't need to be,' he said. 'You're safe now. You're here. With me.'

'I know…but…'

'But what?'

Mikki tried to swallow but her throat felt too tight. 'I can't tell you.'

'Why not?'

She could have said she didn't know. The shock and numbness and confused racing of her brain would have made that true even a few minutes ago but something was becoming very clear to Mikki. Nebulous thoughts were starting to get reined in by talking and things were becoming clearer by the second thanks to the way her hand was enclosed by Tama's. In that strong, sure grip.

'It's just a feeling,' she hedged. 'You wouldn't want to know.'

'Why not?' Tama repeated.

'Girly stuff. I'm not even sure I could put it into words.'

'Try.' Tama's fingers moved over hers. A stroke that was as encouraging as his tone.

Mikki tried to think. If she could put more of it into words, maybe she would understand it better herself. And did it matter if Tama didn't want to hear it? She'd really failed this time and she wasn't sure if she even wanted to try and redeem herself. Maybe this job wasn't what she'd been searching for after all.

'Cheating death,' she said finally. 'It's exciting because of how you feel when you succeed. When you know you're safe.'

'The feeling you didn't get today.'

'But I did. I got it when you came down and got hold of me. When you had your arms around me and I knew

I wasn't going to fall. But as soon as we got up to the chopper and you let me go, the feeling disappeared and I felt scared again.'

She took a shaky breath. 'It was a different kind of safe. I've felt it before with you. When you got me out of that underwater cage and up to the surface of that diving pool. And when we were in that snow mound like two little dots in a place so big we were invisible. It's a feeling I got from you—not from just knowing I wasn't going to die.'

'From when I was holding you?' A chair scraped. 'Like this?'

And Mikki was being drawn up. Held in Tama's arms. Tears were very close. 'Yes.'

'You feel safe now?'

Mikki nodded, her face against his shoulder. She couldn't speak.

Tama's hold tightened. 'But you're shaking. You're still scared.'

'Because it's not real,' Mikki blurted.

'Of course it's real.' She could feel Tama's lips moving against her hair. 'Feel it, Mikki. I'm here and I've got you and it's real, babe.'

Mikki shook her head, her nose rubbing on Tama's chest. 'No. I'm going away and the only way I'll ever feel like this again is by remembering this so it'll never be *real*.'

'You mean real like a real relationship? When you care a lot about what happens to someone?'

Her nose rubbed in the other direction again. Up and down.

'I cared about what was happening to you today,' Tama growled. 'I cared so much I've never been so scared in my life. I thought I was going to lose you. Never be able to hold you again.'

'Don't stop holding me, Tama.'

'I don't intend to.' The words were a murmur. 'Not until you want me to, anyway.'

'Why would I want you to?'

'I mean when you go.'

'Oh…' But why would she want to go anywhere if Tama was here to hold her?

'What is it?' Had Tama sensed her confusion?

'Why do I feel so safe when you're holding me like this? Like you…' She couldn't say it. Couldn't utter a word that had never crossed Tama's lips. One that would instantly conjure up all the kinds of expectations he had said he would never want. She wouldn't see him for dust.

'Like I love you?'

Mikki's heart stopped for a beat. As though she needed to be very, very still so as not to break something precious.

'Is this how it feels?' Tama queried softly. 'Does being in love mean caring so much about someone? Being scared if they're in trouble? Being prepared to risk your own life because you can't bear the thought of being without them?'

'That's weird.' So many impressions were crowding back on Mikki. 'That's what I was wondering when I watched you being winched down to that fishing boat.'

'Did you figure it out?'

'I thought I had. I thought I would get over it because we both knew this wasn't going to last right from the start. That was what made it OK. And that even if I missed you when I went away it would be all right because we could stay in touch with email or something and maybe see each other again one day. But I was wrong.'

Mikki had to pull back to see Tama's face properly. 'I was *so* wrong. It wouldn't be enough just to know you were alive. I need to see that for myself. Every day. To see you and hear you and…and touch you.'

'So is that a "yes"? Is that what it's like to be in love?'

Things were so clear now. 'Yes,' Mikki said quietly. 'Sorry, Tama. I didn't mean to.'

'What?'

'Fall in love with you.'

'It's OK.' But Tama was frowning. He seemed to be collecting his thoughts. 'Listen. I heard you talking to that boy today and I thought you were talking about me. That bit about being too scared to let yourself love someone. Pretending you don't. I'm good at that. So good I believed myself totally. Until today.'

He pulled Mikki close again and dropped his head to rest against hers. 'It's too late not to feel scared of losing you. I'm in too deep. I'm not sure how it happened but it has and, dammit, Mikki—I'm scared now.'

Mikki stretched her arms so they would fit around this big, powerful man whose strength and courage and humour had won her admiration and respect so totally. She tried to hold him so that he wouldn't feel scared. So he would feel safe—like she did when he was holding her.

'Nothing's frightened me since I was a little kid and the worst happened when my mother abandoned me. I've fought ever since and made damn sure I protected myself from ever feeling scared of that kind of thing again. I've never let anyone have the power to really hurt me. But you…' Tama's voice trailed off. There was a tremble in it. 'I never thought I'd ever say this to anyone but you have it, Mikki. You have the power to destroy me.'

'No.' Mikki pulled her arms free so that she could reach up and touch Tama's face. 'I could never do that. I could never hurt you, Tama. I…love you.'

It was one thing to admit to falling in love. Quite another to utter those three, astonishingly powerful little words.

So scary. For a moment, Mikki had the sensation of being in freefall. As though she'd fallen off that cliff she'd been on only a short time ago.

Except she couldn't fall because Tama's arms were still there. Holding her. His head bent further and his lips sought hers and for quite some time there was no need for any further spoken words.

Quite enough was being said.

Asked and promised.

Let go.

There were no ground rules this time. They were both in freefall but they would both be safe if they cared about each other. Held each other.

Tama finally pulled back.

'Just don't ever do that to me again,' he growled. 'Scare me like you did today.'

'It's not like I'm going to get the chance. I failed, didn't I?'

'Hardly. It was a great job. Wasn't your fault the ledge crumbled.'

'You mean I passed? I've qualified? You wouldn't try and stop me doing another job?'

'I can't stop you. Doesn't mean I *want* you to keep doing it, though. Don't ever think you have to try and kill yourself to get me to notice you. Or to get me to tell you that…'

Mikki held her breath.

'That I love you.'

Mikki held Tama's gaze to make absolutely sure she could believe what she was hearing.

Then she let the words sink in for another long, blissful moment. To seep into every cell of her body and make them sing.

Then her lips curved. 'I'm starting to think I might look for a different job. Or go back to my old one. Keep my feet on the ground.' Her smile widened. 'My father's going to really approve of you, Tama James.'

'Not if he hears too much about what happened today.'

'I'll tell him you saved my life. No.' Mikki's smile faded and she held Tama's gaze. 'I'll tell him you *are* my life.'

Tama's face was as serious as her own. 'We're the same, you and me, aren't we? It's more than being in love. It's being…'

'Soulmates?' Mikki suggested.

'Bit girly,' Tama growled. Then he grinned. 'But it'll do. Whatever means that we belong together.' He gathered Mikki close again. So close she could feel his heart beating as strongly as her own. 'Just like this.'

Mikki's echo was a sigh of contentment. 'Just like this,' she agreed.

THE ROYAL HOUSE OF KAREDES

Two crowns, two islands, one legacy

Volume One
BILLIONAIRE PRINCE,
PREGNANT MISTRESS
by Sandra Marton

Wanted for her body – and her baby!

Aspiring New York jewellery designer Maria Santo
has come to Aristo to win a royal commission.

Cold, calculating and ruthless, Prince Xander
Karedes beds Maria, thinking she's only sleeping
with him to save her business.

So when Xander discovers Maria's pregnant,
he assumes it's on purpose. What will it take for this
billionaire prince to realise he's falling in love
with his pregnant mistress…?

Available 17th April 2009